Steve Hussy worked in shithole bars for years before training to be a teacher. He taught for 20 years in colleges and universities, predominantly in the South-East of England.

Hussy formed Murder Slim Press in 2005. 'The Savage Kick' – MSP's literary magazine – was one of the launching pads for best-selling authors Mark SaFranko and Tony O'Neill.

'The Savage Kick' has also published a number of established writers and artists, including: Dan Fante, Joe R. Lansdale, Jim Goad, Doug Stanhope, Joe Matt, Debbie Drechsler, J.R. Helton, Seymour Shubin, Ivan Brunetti, u.v. ray, Carson Mell, Robert McGowan and Willy Vlautin.

When not busy editing or doing design work, Steve Hussy writes stories. His previous works include 'Steps,' 'Back' and numerous stories in magazines printed internationally.
In amongst the booze-driven philosophising, many of them contain rants and scatological gags.

Ah, let's be honest, all of them do...

ACADEMIC

Copyright © 2020 Steve Hussy
All rights reserved
ISBN: 9798655477773

Academic is presented as a work of fiction and any likeness to any person living or dead is entirely coincidental.

10 9 8 7 6 5 4 3 2 1
First Printing

Cover and Interior Art © 2020 Steve Hussy

No part of this book may be used or reproduced in any manner whatsoever without written permission from the publisher, except in the case of quotations embodied in critical articles and reviews.

For all queries contact:
Murder Slim Press,
Sycamore Cottage,
Mill Road,
Burgh Castle,
Norfolk.
NR31 4QS
United Kingdom

Published by Murder Slim Press 2020
www.murderslim.com

Printed in the UK by the MPG Books Group, King's Lynn.

The problem was you had to keep choosing between one evil or another, and no matter what you chose, they slice a little bit more off you, until there was nothing left.

At the age of 25 most people were finished.

Charles Bukowski, Ham On Rye

I only had one life, and I'd be damned if I'd live it in a way that would make me unhappy and please somebody else. I had already lived that kind of life, too much of it already.

Larry Brown, Big Bad Love

Foreword
by Tony O'Neill

The splatter of vomit against concrete. The dull grunts of sad, lonely men screwing bored drunken women. The squeaking springs of filthy beds in decaying rooming-houses. In the hands of Steve Hussy these mundane, everyday sounds become poetry. Music.

Academic knocked me sideways the first time I read it, and further reads diminished none of its power. To read *Academic* for the first time is to experience the thrill and disgust of real human emotion, to see the absurdities at the heart of all relationships revealed under the spotlights glare.

It may not be a comforting journey, but it's a rewarding one, and one packed full of pathos, black humour and sentences that resonate like shrapnel bombs. It's the kind of writing that can only be borne from real pain, real emotion and real life. The only kind of writing that matters.

Tony O'Neill
New York, 2020

ACADEMIC BYSTANDERS SHOULDN'T BE YELLED AT

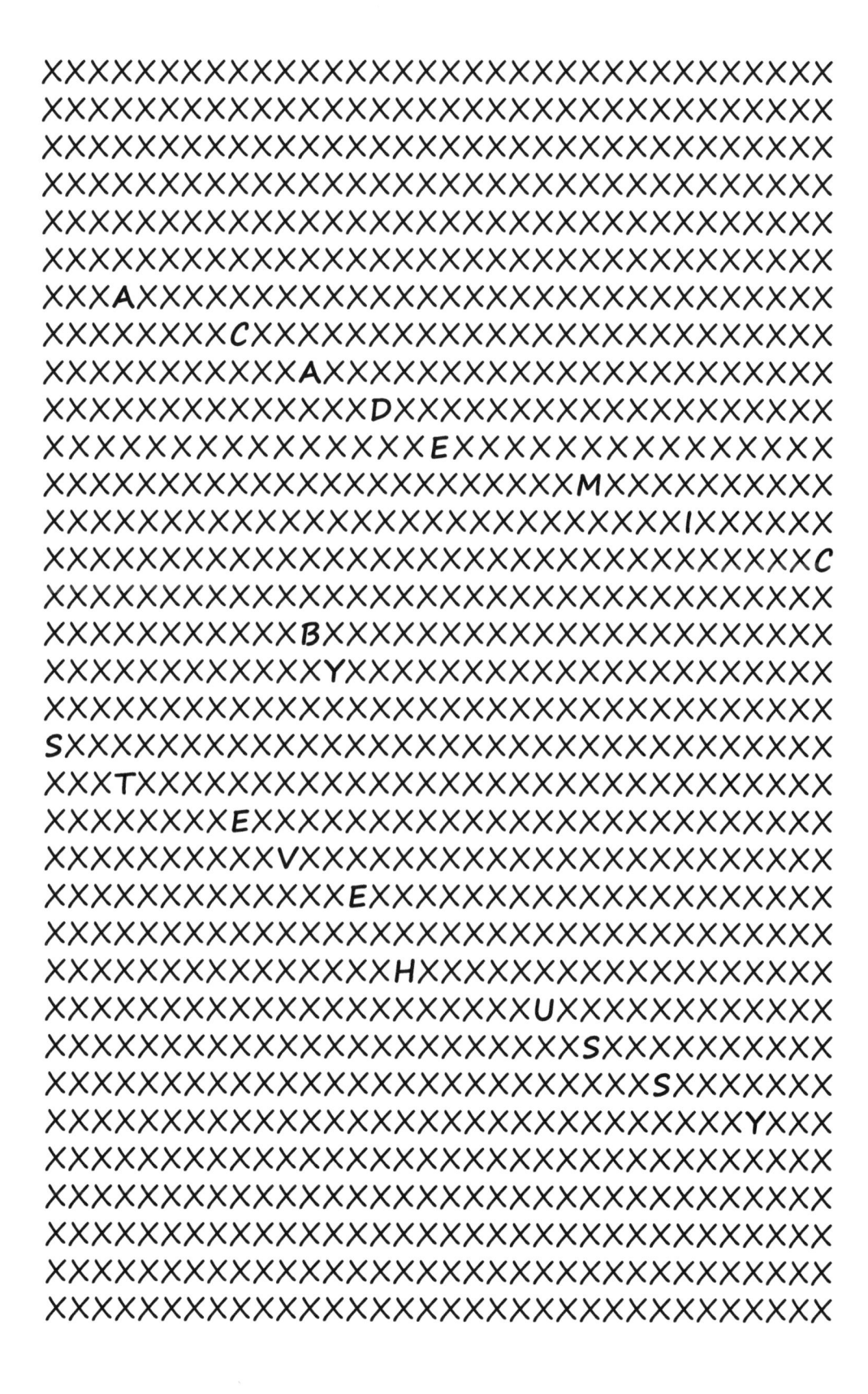

Academic
by Steve Hussy

1

Working in that bar started it. Everything that rumbles around in my brain began there. It's always there when I'm asleep and it's often there when I'm awake.

All that I've learned needs to be controlled or killed. I don't know which is best, but writing about it might help me.

Back then, I was 21 and I had to drink heavily to comfortably slide through time.

The bar I worked in was linked to a holiday camp. I served people whose idea of a holiday was to spend their time with the same people in the same country with the same comfort of normality. Those folks felt they were *away* – a notion reinforced by staying in shithole chalets.

There were the rare great people, but trying to keep the rest happy with booze was like firefighting with kerosene.

And where were the women? Unfortunately, I learned that no right-minded and good-looking woman would visit the holiday camp when they could get a vacation funded by a decent job or a loose-pocketed guy.

Academic

This meant that pleasure was limited to the borderline illegal yet highly developed daughter of a fuckwit: "Can I 'ave an Archers 'n' lemonade?"

She would be 16 and wearing a short skirt with "ANGEL" written across her backside. She would have overblown make-up that destroyed a perfectly decent face and mind.

I'd look quizzically at her: "Are you sure you're old enough?" and she would grow alarmed.

She'd lean over the bar and bare some already yellowing teeth: "Err... puh-leeeese?" Her cleavage would be presented on a Wonderbra shelf.

And, of course, I would say: "You wanna double?"

35 hours a week in that bar, watching the repeating stereotypes. There was a crushing feeling of always having my low expectations lived up to.

With each lad and ladette, each obese wife and dead-eyed father, I knew I needed something new and alive.

Cynicism is mostly laziness but in that bar it was all there was. It was time given and time wasted to buy space elsewhere.

The only upside was there was a dirty truth that made my eyes bulge and soak in everyone's lives. It taught me to watch and listen. The promise of something was always possible, even as I got back to the boarding house after I clocked off at midnight.

Ms. Devgan would be there most nights cleaning the lobby and watching out: "Hi baby!"

She smiled and her bright, almost orange eyes flitted around: "You ok?" She was in the ground-floor flat behind a tapestry screen that she had crafted herself: "How has your tummy been? You looked so pale, I could see it yeah?"

"Hey," my voice hurried, "I'm ok, honestly."

"Here, baby," Ms. Devgan shuffled into her kitchen then popped out again, "take this." It was a little baggie of ginger.

"Thanks," I said, "you didn't have to."

She looked at me slyly: "Come here, baby." I went closer. "Emma's got a boy tonight so be careful ok, yeah?"

"Ok, Ms. Devgan."

"Night, baby."

She loved mothering the people there. We were all young, travelling, or doing some part-time university course. She watched proceedings and didn't intrude. That was usually a mark of class.

There must have been some part of her where she felt she was keeping the riff-raff out. I didn't have the heart to tell her that they were already in...

I creaked up the sticky staircase with its thinning carpet.

When I went into the shared toilet: "AH!" came out of me.

Emma was riding some fat dick in the tub.

He looked astonished and said one, slurred word: "Uhhh?"

He was monged out with wide eyes and flabby features.

Emma turned and smiled at me: "Hey Steve!"

Academic

Emma was a pretty blonde 20-year-old, and she had kind lips and eyes. Unfortunately, my eyes focussed on Emma's giant and pimpled duck-ass peeking out from under her shiny black top.

I had seen all of her body before when she would drink with me in her large and lacy underwear. This time I couldn't see any other forbidden skin, just that backside she jutted out and wobbled as she walked.

"Want me to shut the door?" I asked.

They nodded in unison and I shut it.

I pissed in the stall. Halfway through my waterfall I heard Emma and her boyfriend fucking away again.

It was dry, noisy and frantic.

It sounded like the creaking stairs.

2

Living in the boarding-house wasn't all bad.

Ms. Devgan cleaned the shared toilet facilities with a fanatical pride. You might catch a stray pubic hair if you showered in the morning, but mostly you were secluded and safe.

I usually pissed in my room anyway, and that room is 12 by 12 of detail stored in my insane mind. It was the cheapest I could find in the area but it was plenty good enough. A decent bed, no rats and only the occasional cockroach.

There were flame-marks riding up the right-hand wall and stains on the shit brown carpet. But all that was offset by having my own sink. It was good enough to piss and jerk off into.

I liked the set-up. It was my own primordial cave.

I'd lay down in my bed and feel something *different*, some knowledge that my brain was misaligned. I would pull the whiskey to my mouth and let it slide down as I stared at the ceiling. I enjoyed the burn, but I wished it would extend to my synapses.

"Why did I say that?" I'd ask myself over something trivial at the bar. "What if you did this?" I would analyse microscopic moments until my stomach churned.

I took some of the ginger from Ms. Devgan's baggie, and then the bats started to crawl above in the attic. I'd hear them talking to each other chitterchitterchitter and crawling over each other and fucking away with their chitterchitterchitterchitter.

The incessant noise lasted until six in the morning. I didn't know how many were up there, but it felt like thousands. I'd open the mud brown curtains and watch the dark angular forms flying erratically, while the rest still chitterchitterchittered away, above, below, around, and sometimes just in my head.

My mind would crawl with them as in the room below someone would start fucking.

The bed would creak or they would pound against the door. Some movie poster rustled in between each thrust. Stroke, rustle, stroke, rustle. Erg Erg Erg Oooo Erg Erg Ahhhhhhhhhhhhh…

Academic

There were so many quick, desperate fucks among those quick, desperate people.

I had to keep trying to sleep and knock down all the chittering with whatever I could find. I was a child lost in the dark, swimming in the shit of the stupid need created by loneliness.

I had a voice that was tired of my right hand and yet I was tired of the other voice berating my brain. I disliked my feelings. They twisted my cynicism, but they were there and they screamed.

Concentrate chitter-ahhh concentrate chitter-erg CONCENTRATE chitter-aaaaah mmmmmmmm...

3

I first heard him through the wall. He was masturbating and talking to his cock: "Come on, come on, COME ON."

The walls were thin enough to smell his cum. I listened to my personal stereo to drown it the noise, but it didn't work. My hearing uncontrollably hooked onto the strange and awful.

"Yeah, yeah that's it," and then he shouted, "YEAH!"

I tried to avoid contact. I used the shared kitchen and the shared toilet as little as possible, but I needed human contact. I had beaten it down but Homo-erectus is a social animal...

I met him in the kitchen as I was cooking pasta. My microwave couldn't manage that. It was 12.30pm. I'd got back from work and felt the hunger and booze pangs. My red wine was already open.

"Hi," I said, feeling myself shrink and wanting to sink into a silent, black sleep. "I'm Steve."

"Hey dere," a middle-American accent, "it's Brad."

Brad extended a hand. He was tall and muscular, and I was easily big enough to look evenly into his fixed grey-blue eyes.

I asked: "You want a drink?"

Back then, I'd drink a couple of bottles of wine a day or a half-bottle of spirits.

He said: "Sure."

We went back to his room. It was the same shaped box as mine but cleaner. He had a few books on the shelves and a tapestry on the wall. There was incense burning and an army-style kit bag in the corner.

Brad asked: "What do you do?" It was the question everyone wants to know.

"I'm training to be a teacher." He gave no response to that. "What're you doing?"

"Ah'm travellin' thru Europe. Doing some writin' here for the year too."

"Where've you been?"

"Here," and he finally smiled, "and there."

We talked for an hour after that. He had stories about Italy, France and Spain. Like me, he wanted to go to Scandinavia next.

He said: "The wimmen dere 'posed to be hot as hell."

"Yet the place is as cold as here."

He smiled again: "Weather makes 'em grow up sexy to survive."

He had a half-bottle of bourbon and shared it happily. I chugged another shot: "What'd you do... before now?"

"I was a Marine," Brad said.

"Yeah?" The first Iraq War had been only a few years before: "You were in the Gulf?"

"Yeah."

"What'd you do?"

"Everyone ax that." Now he narrowed his eyes: "Ah worked comms. Keepin' stuff together. Nuttin' much, no fightin'."

"Did you see anything?"

His fixed grey-blue eyes stared: "Everyone ax that too."

"Do they?"

"We worked cleanup." He shut his eyes: "Bodybaggin', that shit. So ah saw shit. One guy in a cab, jus' the top half of 'im. Other half was layin' in the road."

My mouth opened but nothing came out.

He opened his eyes and went on: "We had to shovel 'em up. Had these little fold-out shovels. Then we stick 'em in the same bag, y'know?"

The images filled my brain. How had he survived such horror? As ever, my eyes were wide and unblinking.

I wasn't any good with conversation. I tried to listen more than talk, but then words raised up and I'd think I had said the wrong thing. I sensed people's feelings and put them onto myself.

"Ya wan' 'nother drink?" Brad asked.

That woke me up: "Yeah... thanks."

He poured it, I drank it, and then I listened some more.

4

Ms. Devgan's nephew was staying in the boarding-house. He was on holiday from India, but working as a locum to fund it.

That night her nephew screamed: "OH HELP ME PLEASE I AM DYING!" in the corridor as Brad and I walked past him.

We looked at each other, moved on by, got into Brad's room and he locked his door. Brad then said: "Shit."

"Hmm."

Brad poured a drink for me. That night we had tequila slammers from a cheapo litre bottle, along with slices of lemon and salt. The shots fizzed in my brain, but not in my voice.

I asked: "Shouldn't we go and help him?"

"He's jus' drunk," Brad said evenly, "lettum figure it out for hisself..."

"OH HELP ME PLEASE!" Dr. Singh screamed again.

"Isn't Ms. Devgan about?"

"Nope... ah checked her room earlier," Brad looked towards his sink, "ah guess she's with her son." He downed the next shot: "Fuck knows."

I said: "She told me he was a doctor..." as her nephew wailed some more outside.

"Yeah... Sikhs don't drink." He laughed: "Guess he's been a bad black boy!"

I took another drink to process that without wanting to hit Brad. Then Dr. Singh said: "Oh help me please!" a little softer.

There was yet more drinking before we heard Emma's door open. She came out and comforted him for a while.

Emma said: "Are you ok?"

"NO! I AM DYING!"

A pause, then a near-silence. She must have hugged him, but she left after he didn't respond with anything except moans.

Ah, ah, ah...

"So ya lookin' forward ta teachin'?" Brad asked.

"I need a career." Now I was the one with narrowed eyes: "And I think I can do it."

Brad downed a slammer then filled my glass. "Ya sound as sure as you ever do." There was sarcasm in his tone of voice...

I wet between my thumb and forefinger. He poured the salt over it and I drank the tequila and it fizzed away. I didn't have many answers. The booze helped but the interior questions would still churn my stomach.

There was a pause as we drank and thought. Singh started to whisper, still stomping up and down. We could hear his feet but they were much slower now: "Oh help me please."

I asked: "Where are you gonna travel to next?"

"Here, You-rope, Japaaaan," Brad's voice slurred, "Shit, wherever mah mood takes me. Marines weren't 'nough."

"You miss home?"

"Fuck no. My father iz so fuckin' religious." I couldn't discern whether Brad was too. "Ah needed to get 'way. Thaz why ah joined th' Marines. To see stuff..." He poured another shot of tequila. "Ah didn't even FUCK at home, y'know? Ah did it first with a Filipino." Then he laughed again: "Paid ten dollars to a whore. She was a good l'il gal an' she did mah cleanin' fer a week."

We sat for another minute or so, listening to the Singh's moans gradually softening.

"i am dying.... help me please..."

Brad broke the near silence. "Mah old man got crazy once over th' Armageddon, an' ah mean he got *convinced*. He went inna garage an' boarded it up. Stocked it up with canned goods," he laughed, "an' all that kool-aid, fer fuck's sake!"

I was blinking and unblinking my eyes to focus them: "What's kool-aid?"

"Iz just pop fer stupid people." He took a long slug of tequila. "Mom wasn't into any of it. Shit! Pop's face the day it was s'posed to come an' him lookin' outta there dreamin' of a fuckin' apocalypse." His smile had a pang of something else to it.

There was quiet again as Singh whispered outside: "oh help me..."

"You listen ta this," Brad said. He passed me his Walkman and I stuck in an earphone.

I heard: "Baby, I think of you a lot ya know? Like today, like I was listenin' to Pat Metheny and I thought of you." She continued to drone about her day. She worked in a vet's. She lived on her own but had hung out with friends.

"Cassie," he said as his dead grey-blue eyes glazed a little.

"She sounds nice," I said, feeling the weight of expectation. I felt a voice whispering "average" but said: "Are you with her?"

"We split 'fore ah left. Ah guess iz complicated." Another dreamy look with the hint of a smile. "She's *beautiful*. She's only 18. Ah dunno. She's *smart* too y'know... She's grown up now."

"Yeah?"

"Yeah..." he thought a little more. "Yeah, she has... Man, she's fuckin' beautiful, y'know?"

Singh was directly outside the door. He whispered: "oh I am dying... I am dying..."

Then he started to vomit: "HOOOOOOOROARGH!"

"Shit!" said Brad.

The puke pounded against the door and then Dr. Singh must have wheeled around.

"HWAAAARGH," he heaved, "HOOOOURAAAG. HOO-HOO-HORRRRRRRRRRRG."

Brad started laughing but I was transfixed, looking at the closed door.

"He's fuckin' goin' for it!" Brad said loudly over it.

"HUH-HUH-HUH-HUH..." He was coughing out there, but was he choking?

"Shit!" said Brad, for the umpteenth time. "Ah better go..."

Brad got up and opened the door and a mound of thick puke greeted him. The stench hit me and I stood up. I reeled and veered towards the wall. I bounced towards my apartment.

I looked left and saw Brad leading Dr. Singh through his door. My vision slid to the right, and that made me veer to the left. I just avoided some more puke before I fumbled with my key in the lock, and felt it all build inside.

I got the key around, went in, turned on the light and locked the door. I spun around to the sink and it hammered out...

"HARGOUGH," I was trying to keep it quiet but it hacked out anyway. Brown and thick, rising up at me and filling the sink.

"HOROUGH." Another load of acrid brown shit. Even in the mayhem in my fevered head, I thought "Why's it not going down?"

"HUH-HOROUGH," another load. No, no, no, it lurched up at me again, two thirds full now. That fucking chocolate pudding earlier. I vomited again at the sickly sweet stench of it.

I reached down into it with my right hand. It was warm, wetter on top and thicker further down. I got my fingers into the plughole and started pushing the solid bits through. I heaved at that as well, but came up emptier each time.

I dry heaved for ten minutes, whispering "fuck, fuck, fuck" in caught breaths. But something had been born inside me...

I brushed my teeth to try to calm it down but I hacked that up too.

Then I started to laugh. A big gut laugh wheezed out through my bile burned throat.

This was utter nonsense... but it helped to teach me how to think like a fucking adult and accept that shit is everywhere.

5

My teaching trainer's coo-coo one-note voice rattled in my skull. She excitedly asked: "Has anyone had a go at writing on the whiteboard?!"

She was perfectly average in every way. Another nonentity floating to her grave. Draw your own picture of her...

She said: "Let's have a go at it!"

The training involved crowing super-eager child-adults guiding confused wide-eyed child-adults how to teach. Yet there I was sitting wide-eyed and unable to say how unremittingly stupid everything was.

I was caught between feeling and the daily grind. I needed a qualification to get a full-time job, but I had a psychotic need for reality too.

I'd smell my own booze funk around me and the paraffin fumes from my mouth. I'd feel dizzy on them and yet they made me happy. They helped me tolerate the world, as did the knee-booted woman across from me in the circle of the seminar.

"It can be a bit hard," the trainer went on, "but it'll be wonderful practice!"

I peered down at the fellow student's calves in those boots. Mmm... a little heel and a little tone.

Someone said: "How about you? How are you getting on?"

The boots' wearer was repellent in every other way, but those boots and her slivers of her calves were peeking out from her just-over-the-knee length skirt...

Some voice again: "Hello?"

My damned brain never saved my cock. I remembered some of the vicious bile the knee-booted woman had spouted. I knew that her legs would be flabby and hairy. The boots gave them more than she had. But still...

"HELLO?"

I looked up at the trainer's eyes.

"Oh, sorry." I attempted an innocent little grin.

"Would you like to have a go on the whiteboard?"

"Alright." It felt like sacrilege to disappoint her.

Academic

"Don't worry if you struggle a bit!" Her face smiled but her voice didn't. "We're all in the same boat!"

"..." I couldn't speak although I knew she wanted reassurance. I had used the whiteboard a thousand times before at my part-time teaching gig.

I stood and wrote in my too-hurried script: *"Laura Mulvey was an important film critic who explored the vile nature of..."* and the tutor started to babble: "Good, good! Oh! You're getting better!" My writing neatened up, but I wanted to stick my forefingers in my ears. She said: "That's excellent! Well done you!"

The other people clapped and the knee-booted woman crossed her legs.

I did that task and all of the others they foisted on me. One Saturday a month, 9am to 5pm. There was an hour break in the middle where I'd go the toilets to eat and top up on some booze.

Then I would rush home to my room and to peace. I had stacks of books that I had been poring over for the previous years.

Brad had lent me *Post Office* first, then *Ask The Dust*. I'd got on the internet after that. I picked up *Pimp, Hangover Square*, and more Bukowski and Fante. Later I expanded to Hamsun, Tanizaki, Dostoevsky, Trantino, Celine, Himes, Mrabet and on and on...

I read slowly and soaked in every line. These new worlds and these crazy people.

Academic

I'd also scour the net to find movies on video and DVD. I'd gained a bitter taste for hitmen, serial killer movies and film noir: *Henry*, *The Third Man*, *Seven*, *Blast of Silence*, *The Night of the Hunter*, *Dark City*, *Touch of Evil*, *The Vanishing*.

The Vanishing was my favourite. The character of Rex. He was a sociopath who had horror enforced on him. He had to prove his love and drink the drugged coffee.

Of course, the sadistic Chemistry teacher Raymond didn't die at the end and Rex was buried alive...

6

Weeks on, I was eating tomato soup in the kitchen with Erica. Brad had shared a 69 with her one night. He said: "Ah was jus' drunk," but the dirty truth was that he wanted pussy and any wet hole would do.

Erica was an American too, a foghorn with a Californian drone. She wasn't exactly fat but she was big and tall with a pignose, watery lips and cold eyes.

"Eeeee-yew!" she wailed. "I can't believe you didn't buy HEINZ."

"These were cheaper."

"I," and she dragged out that I, "only buy *brand* names."

I kept eating, unsure of how I could get her to stop talking.

"Ya know," she said to fill the air, "I had my period today and it's like so weeee-ird..." Her snout crinkled up: "It's all like... sticky, ya know?"

I studied her face. It was empty of anything except mild, snide arrogance. "It's all black," Erica said, "all yukky and gloopy... ya know?"

A crystal clear image manifested... I was pulling down her idiot head into my soup and holding it there. Her hands tried to scratch me as I watched the bubbles rise until she became limp.

Then I thought myself evil and said: "Must be pretty rough for you."

I felt scared of my insanity. Too much and too hard. I'd be surprised by it but I still kept turning the pages of life.

As I watched the crazies in movies and books and life, there were louder whispers: "Yeah, yeah, this is right. This is IT."

7

Lanny came next, with her beautiful pale brown skin.

Before Lanny, I masturbated to big-titted porn I found online. The action I had got before that were fumbled kisses and a handjob when I was 16. That had been followed by a lovely looking psychopath who I dated when we were both 17.

The relationship with Emma lasted for a furious six weeks. Her insistence on listening to the 120 beats-by-minute drone of dance music like "Slipmatt" during sex had made my stroke all too fast. By the second week, I had learned how to control my cock. All I had to do was push down the muscle above my hard-on. After that, we would end up in a beautiful and sweaty mess.

I got acne vulgaris just after the break-up with Emma. It was all over my face and back. Was this some reaction to missing her? Some kind of embodiment of my idiot brain? All I knew was the pus put off women for a while.

I was prescribed Roaccutaine and it had worked... I had pristine skin again. Sadly, it also drove some people nuts. The common side effects were insomnia and unnecessary rages. The most profoundly affected by Roaccutaine committed suicide.

They banned the drug a few years later. I'm still here to tell this tale, but maybe the acne scars had soaked into my brain.

Lanny was certainly sweet and attractive enough to soothe all of those scars. As a physiotherapist, she may well have been built for the task.

She had a slight overbite and I loved the way it looked when she smiled. Lanny was cute, tall, toned and athletic. She moved with energy and a smile, a beautiful accompaniment to her quick-witted voice.

Ah. No. Shit, why I am writing something that makes me remember her again? I, I, I... remember and why can't I forget? Her dark brown eyes were so *alive*. They flicked around and looked as if they were soaking her own reality into her. She had true intelligence and a love of being goofy.

Academic

Brad had met her in the post-graduate bar at our university. Lanny was a physio and nearing the end of her training. She was suffering yet more lectures and essays, all dovetailed with work placements.

I met her in Brad's room. It was a gathering with him and some other Americans.

"Ya know he could hear me jerkin' off..." Brad poked a thumb at me.

The other Americans were struck dumb, but the booze helped my line pop out: "I liked to join in... I'd get so hard."

"Dreeeeeeee..." Lanny's laugh leaked out through clenched teeth, while the Americans stared at two crazy Brits.

Brad said: "I heard ya... I'd cum jus' thinkin' 'bout you."

Lanny exploded into a plummy, horselike wheezing laugh: "uuuuuh-HAAAAAAH, uuuuh-HAAH!"

Everyone else drew back, but I loved her then. All too much and all too quickly. Energy is infectious.

Lanny wanted Brad, and that was fair enough. He was confident and muscular. He was the perfect fuck. I was the sidekick with the odd decent line but generally I was just odd.

Despite my size, my body language showed it. I was withdrawn, hunched, twitchy...

Lanny stayed with Brad that first night. The next day he told me she had given him a massage: "Said she needed ta practice..."

She had got her tits out, oiled them up and rubbed them down his back. But he couldn't follow through. They slept together with no sex of any kind.

"Her tits, they were... Ah dunno, sorta funky?" He preferred women with small breasts. "Lanny's go outta lot." Then he motioned his hands as if to shape them, scrunching up his face in semi-disgust.

I imagined Lanny in a dream. She didn't hold any problems for me other than causing an uncomfortable erection in the morning and a need for her to brighten my confusing world.

8

Brad dismissed Lanny because he was too hung up on Cassie. She was still working as a veterinary assistant in Kansas City. He would ogle the few photographs he had of her.

"Lookit," he said, and carefully passed them to me. Her eyes looked somewhat dead, but she had beautiful curly hair.

Brad would duck out of our drinking sessions to have late-night phone conversations with Cassie. This was before the days of mobile phones, so he'd stand dutifully in a phone box for an hour and then come back sheepishly.

His grey-blue eyes started to show some life. He talked more and he organised his trip back to the USA.

He quit his part-time Creative Writing course two months early, and left two weeks later. He caught a bus to the airport to catch a plane back to Cassie. "She's the love of mah life," he said with his new, almost sinister smile.

Lanny and I walked him to the bus station. I could see she was crestfallen. She bubbled around more than ever to try to hide it: "Youse better write arr oi'll kick y'awl ass," she said, with a fake American drawl.

"Sure," Brad said with now only almost-dead eyes.

He shook my hand and hugged her. Then he got on the coach and left.

He didn't look back.

Lanny came back to my room to drink. It was like a wake... a mourning. It felt lovely – if terrifying – to be around her alone. I drank more while she spoke so fast her words tumbled out: "And then I was just drinking and drinking and dancing on the table for everyone and smashing the plates really fucking well then KERCHING like fell off and fell on the floor and my ankle went OUT and I think I passed out and got carried back to the bed." Then her giant smile, with a voice that remained classy to a hick like me: "And I woke up I dunno when it was I woke up I guess it was the night it was dark and I was covered in water or something fucking wet you know – SOAKED – what's up with that?"

"You sure it was water?"

"Dreeeeee..."

Academic

We drank four and a half bottles of wine over six ridiculous hours filled with almost constant laughter, poking and prodding at each other physically and mentally.

Lanny was pissed after two bottles, and I was gone after four. Lines would pop out of my mouth throughout the drinking session. Half-stolen, half-remembered words from people much smarter than myself. I'd added plagiarism to my limited skills.

"Y'know," I said, "*Pulp Fiction* is a gritty urban satire?"

She pouted her lips: "Yeah..."

"Well *Pump Friction* is about people having dry, dirty sex."

She laughed her wheezing laugh. I couldn't focus long enough to figure it all out. The wine meant the time slided over me and that separation felt nice.

She ended up sitting between my legs on the floor. I started stroking her straightened deep-auburn hair. It felt calming, like stroking a cat. My cock strained against the back of her head.

She looked up at me from there and smiled. She staggered as she got up then righted herself with a bodypop shrug.

Lanny pulled her top over her head, then she pulled her sports bra down over her midriff. Her tits did hang out to the side and they were a lot bigger than I'd dreamed. She had large areolas and her nipples were oh-so-dark and oh-so-beautiful.

"Oops!" she said and smiled. "I done did popped out!"

Her smile was even more beautiful than her breasts. I was addicted to smiles and there had to be truth in the way she then stroked my head and asked: "Are you ok?" with her perfect teeth and body and brain.

I concentrated on not saying anything. I didn't want to fuck up. Then that thought was gone too and I slid back into it all.

"I'm more than that," was the best I could manage. I looked up at her and smiled.

"Good," Lanny said. "Jus' dun' tell Brad 'bout this," and the hilarity of that line struck me months later and again as I write it.

9

Lanny visited every four days or so. Drunk, half-drunk, or ready to drink. There was usually some party she wanted me to take her to. House parties, student parties, NHS parties... mostly a bunch of people in a pub pissing their time away.

I smiled at jokes but never managed many laughs. I made small talk but did it badly. Everyone looked like they were having fun, so I beat down any original thought and tried to understand her world.

Lanny was an excellent show-woman and the centre of attention. She blasted around with her dancing and goofy jokes. She would squeeze her tits together, pout, laugh, and flirt wildly with me and anyone else around.

One time we played a game of dare. The first guy was dared to take his jeans down. He was a bland trainee nurse who had a dreary voice but wacky Nirvana-esque hair and a striped top. He was fashionable enough to be thought cool.

He said: "No, no, no!" as the table bayed at him.

I took a large slug of cider and I was the only one not chanting: "OFF! OFF! OFF!"

Lanny strutted over to him, and pulled down his sagging jeans. He was wearing blue pants and there was a big wet patch. His dick had been leaking precum over Lanny's tit-squeezing.

That did make me laugh, and Lanny "dreeeee-d" wildly while the rest sat in stunned silence as he ran off to the toilets.

The poor guy shunned us after that... and rightly so.

Another time, Lanny was giving me a blowjob. We were both drunk. I'd happily eaten her pussy and now she was working hard and fast with her hands and her lips. She always attacked my cock with real gusto.

I accidentally shot some cum in her mouth before pulling out: "I'm so fucking sorry!"

She looked up and grinned, "No, no..." Lanny licked her lips: "Mmm... Tastes like HONEY."

She started laughing and after a few seconds I joined in with that too. It felt open and real.

But the memory forever etched is from watching Lanny give a physio demo to some students.

She had practiced on me many times, but the demo needed to be with another physio student.

Lanny asked: "Can you cheer and applaud at the end?"

"Well, yeah, if you want."

"Make it super, super, SUPER sincere." She beamed away as she rubbed the oil on my naked crotch: "They'll be so impressed!"

And so we both moved into acting...

10

Lanny had to narrate her massage to the audience of two lecturers and 20 other students: "The most important aspect here is to work into the muscle fibre." I knew her well enough that she was withholding a smile.

I had got drunk beforehand to ensure I didn't fuck up my role as an audience member. Only a few people on her course knew who I was. She had kept me separate from most of them, and I enjoyed being almost incognito.

I was watching Lanny's tits and I saw her dark nipples starting to raise through her white top. She was so beautiful. It was something about the way her bellybutton showed above her jeans, and the way her white t-shirt contrasted with her skin.

The guy was decent looking, there was a cold draft and her beautiful nipples tended to raise anyway.

She looked so happy that it felt like I was watching my own, true nirvana.

Lanny kept mashing away: "This can relieve various forms of cramping or adhesion caused by stress, mild tears or deterioration."

I coughed repeatedly and eventually got her attention. I nudged my head down at her nipples and winced. Lanny blushed, turned away and started to rub, trying to warm them up. But when she turned back, the oil on her hands had soaked in and her large red-brown nipples shone through.

She looked down and grinned to her audience. She said: "Fuck me, you could tune a radio on these."

The room hushed and I started laughing loudly again.

She was endearing to my warped sense of humour. She gradually drew me out of cynicism and lost me in simple joys.

Lanny theatrically threw everything she had into living. When she danced she flailed, when she played sports she charged, and when she fucked she jerked and screamed.

So when she visited me, I loved the feeling of her crashing through the door: "HEY YOU!" and a smile. A shot of expectation that would be filled.

The booze helped those good times and gave them energy. She wanted to fuck drunk much more than when we were sober. I wanted to fuck all of the time, but the booze made me not shy away from it.

She'd drink and she'd lean back, pull her shirt off, giggle, pull me inside her or down on her. Moan, ahhh, SCREAM. We always made sure we both came, but what I miss more is laying next to her and holding her. The closeness, the softness. The rest I can get from lubing up and curling my hand just right.

I'd lay there and stroke my hand down over her hair, between her breasts, up over her smooth stomach, then down the curve of her thigh. That warm skin, the way it would twitch, the gentle movement of breath.

When you hold someone, they are perfection. Comforting, loving, honest. Ah, ah, Lanny...

It all made me feel something too. Less ugly, less unsure. Being around Lanny made me feel like I could catch her energy, her naturalness, her beauty.

After that, nothing else seemed to matter.

11

Time rushed forward. I would wait for Lanny to appear again at increasingly random periods. 7 days, 3 days, 5 days later.

I felt a dizziness around her. Happiness, delusion, her skin and smiles beating down any thoughts bubbling away.

I don't think it was then when the voices started, but I could feel them getting louder. The interrogations fully came when I was asleep or trying to sleep: "It's so nice... her being around, you love it, you love her, stop fucking your life up, STOP IT STOP IT."

Hints of trouble started to be noticeable. First, when I asked to meet her parents: "Shouldn't I meet them?"

"Nah, don't worry about that!" She laughed her wheezing laugh: "You'd be so bored!"

Again: "What's your place like? You wanna go there instead of this shithole?"

"Nah, I like it here!"

Yet again, as she got dressed, I said: "You know you don't have to leave. I'll stay on the floor if you want the bed..."

"Nah, I like *my* bed!" She pouted and pointed up at the attic: "And those accursed bats... dreeeee!"

She never stayed and she seldom kissed me.

The booze would make me face life too much so I stopped drinking. Then when I was sober the voices would come too quickly so I drank more.

They were all convenient lies to get through to the drug of seeing Lanny again.

Organised thought did slowly filter through. I was too fucked up to do any better and I knew it. Being with Lanny was a fluke, but it had brought arrogance with it: *"I can't fuck skanks, so I'll have to perfect the usual charade. I just have to memorise the lines needed, the body language. Focus, learn it. Learn everything."*

But my damned self-destructive brain again. It even judged Lanny with the shots of life she would give... I found out the problem with wacky people is that it wears thin unless they

Academic

keep going further and further. Now I was reading about Iceberg Slim keeping his stable of prostitutes in line, Knut Hamsun wondering whether a few buttons could drum up enough krone for food, and Patrick Hamilton being torn to pieces by his beloved Netty.

Lanny dancing the Funky Chicken in a "too boring" queue lost its lustre. She needed a new act but I didn't have the guts to say it. I tried to share books with her to broaden her horizons.

"What did you think of *Ham On Rye*?"

"Oh, haha, I couldn't be bothered with it." That beautiful smile yet again: "Sorry, it was too long."

Too long? TOO LONG?

"Yeah, I guess it is little long." I was a liar... a coward... but her smile... oh, if you had seen it you would understand.

No-one thinks they're a simple minded fool. I could say to myself, particularly drunk, that I was better than many of the rest. I tried hard but some disconnected wire in my brain wouldn't let life be. It sensed something in her quiet or when the booze ran out.

Lanny never looked at me with love, she just fucked me and acted her role. I saw it in the way she rarely met my eyes.

It broke out in the most minor of ways. We were watching *The Seventh Seal* and I could see her mind drifting: "You ok?"

"Yeah."

I watched Lanny withdraw a little, then her eyes turn away.

I said: "You sure?"

She looked at the wall. "He never writes to me, you know? Does he write to you?"

Oh no. She was still hung up on Brad: "Yeah. Once..."

The noise in my head became loud enough for me to blurt out another of my lifelong, recurring gems: "What's going on?"

"Huh?" she smiled.

"Us? Lan... What are we? Are we together?" Yet another of my stupid maxims, but my voice was flat. I never shouted any time other than to protect people: "I have no idea."

Why couldn't I shut up? What was wrong with me?

"You think too much," she said, then smiled again.

Pussy and beauty... *Oh, why couldn't I shut the fuck up?*

I started to feel dizzy, then she looked me in the eyes and held them there. Those magical dark-brown eyes.

Lanny said: "You're a real thinker, aren't you?" Her eyes kept looking straight at me and straight inside me. She stroked her right hand through my hair: "Now you're hot, aren't you?"

I looked down. "Nah," I felt the dizziness and nausea grow. I said: "Nah. I'm cool," and I started to sweat.

12

Lanny's physiotherapy training entered the phase where she would be working all of the time. It meant she spent one month in the local hospital, then one month abroad. That continued for six months. It meant she was able to satisfy her wanderlust and I felt excited for her too.

Lan being away for long stretches of time helped us. It gave us time outside the eye of the storm.

Life became just me and the boarding house. We were both strange and isolated edifices... empty voids that needed to be filled.

Emma permanently moved away. Luckily I only saw her spotted ass three more times. She gave me her phone number and said goodbye with a smile and a hug.

A guy named Rob moved into Brad's room. There were no more sounds of jerking off through the wall. Rob was only concerned with real-life ladies. I always saw Rob in a suit or his "lucky pulling shirt." He was short, around 5'5", with his hair in a precise Tintin quiff.

He said: "I'm co-ordinating insurance in the area. I'm a sort of area manager," before I had even asked a question. He couldn't have been co-ordinating much to end up in the bat hotel.

The rest of the tenants were one month lets with offshore workers. My mechanical brain remembers all the names, but they meant nothing. A few words, a pass in the hall, a meal shared in the kitchen.

I needed nothing other than books, movies and Lanny. I'd have a cup of foul-tasting herbal tea with Ms. Devgan and exchange a few words with co-students at my teacher training.

Academic

The nature of the education system meant there was only one other male teacher on my course. He was an angry Journalism teacher trainee in his forties. The rest were fourteen young women. I was on a completely different wavelength from these giggling, chatty, passive-aggressive female teachers-to-be.

"I had the worst lesson ever today," Brown-haired Creature said, "he's a walking turd."

"I know, I know," Red-haired Creature said, "lemme tell you about this little shit in my Year 9 class..."

Ah well... Mostly I had huge periods alone to drink, to read, to think. I had the freedom to watch other people and myself.

At the start of it all, I tried a few bars but I hated them. I wasn't built for society. I didn't want to talk to people, but I was young enough to still feel dizzy if there was silence around me. I had to shoot the shit with these strangers, then I would leave and blearily wonder why I had bothered in the first place.

When I got claustrophobic I would sit outside, especially if it rained. I often sat alone on the hill looking over a lake, watching the rain and listening to the sound of the drops on the leaves and the water.

Other times I'd sit on benches in the bigger parks. People would sit opposite on another bench and I'd feel their gaze. I feigned reading a book. It was a visual aid that said: "STAY AWAY."

I would watch their body language and listen to them talk about shoes, sex and accepted nothingness. I could see people withdraw when they didn't like the other person, but the other person still laboured on. Why couldn't they see it? Why couldn't they hear anything?

"...fuckin' Man U... he's really *complicated* you know... yeah, nought to sixty in 7.2... did you see his *hair*... I mean, yeah, abso-*lute*-ly... his music really, really, really *speaks* to me..."

I saw fat girls with piercings, gel-headed idiotic lads, popular gals, morose male goths, sluts, geezers, cunts and Oasis fan-boys. They were all members of clubs with regulation clothes and hairdos. A normalised way of existing and an antiseptic death.

A country of popular idiots and outsider idiots, oblivious to themselves. And who could blame them? The world welcomed them with open arms.

In the rain, I had my hood up and I lifted a cider bottle to my mouth now and then.

The other people moved on quickly after seeing that. A nutjob was in their midst, and I was only a little better than any of them.

Drink, just fucking DRINK.

And finally my eyes would happily close.

13

Lanny was right. I did think too much.

Academic

The world was an infinite bubble filled with confusing people. I wanted to take my thumb and burst it. Not to hurt anyone – I could never do that – but I wanted to reset how people behaved. It would also resolve how I acted and thought. I had a malformed brain with fucked-up skin stretched over it.

In the pouring rain, I thought back to when I was a kid.

Even at school, I was always odd. I preferred to sit by myself and I froze during class presentations. Yet I could always chug out the work to a high standard and I could ace exams at any level.

Maybe the shit at home prompted it? Or maybe I was born with contorted reasoning? I tried to be normal but something in me always failed at that, no matter how hard I tried.

I remembered my grandfather's funeral when I was 17.

My father's dad had Parkinson's Disease. He moved slowly and he shook a lot, but he was always tuned in. The Parkinson's never addled him and he would respond quickly to questions.

My grandmother had died due to crippling arthritis and the medications needed to try to control it. Somehow he managed to keep going for 12 more years, but he was crushed by her loss.

The tiny vice he developed was to do "little bets" on horse racing. Maybe 10p on a horse each-way, 20p to win if he was feeling certain. 10-15 races per day. He would meticulously break down the form and send my aunt to the betting office.

My father said he still made a decent profit on that. I never knew why he didn't increase his bets. I suspect he was too nice to make a killing.

I loved my grandfather. He had a thick head of white hair and white dandruff on his green corduroy jacket. He smiled a lot with his grey and broken – but still his own – teeth.

His sister, my father and I had been the only people to see him for years. I rarely knew what to say so I'd give him PG-rated stories about my school or college. I smiled and shuffled out agreeable words. He referred to me as "Smiler."

Two of my grandparents had died before I was 5 years old, but he had always been here. Now – after pneumonia – he was nowhere, soon to be forgotten in some hole in the ground. I cried but I knew he would dislike that.

There were 31 people at the funeral. I hadn't seen most of them before. Cousins, uncles, nephews...

The hymns started with "Abide With Me." I was in the centre of the front row. My father was singing, as were the people behind. It was so terrible and so tuneless that I started laughing.

Even through the tears, my uncontrolled little laughs burst out. I tried to keep them back then spurted out another tiny laugh. No-one turned and my father never stopped singing. I hoped no-one had noticed.

At the wake, I drank whisky macs. Almost everyone was drinking, and that made it feel better. The crowd started to flow together rather than apart.

A half-aunt, a niece, who knows, came up and said "Hello." I couldn't decipher the expression on her face: "You're a really smiley sort aren't you? Didn't Fred use to call you 'Smiler'?"

"Yeah," I said, feeling the red rise up and overwhelm me. "Yeah, he did."

"That's so nice." I never saw her again, but I remember how her eyes knotted into something that might have been anger: "That shows how nice you are, doesn't it?"

14

Booze continued to be the way to keep going when Lanny wasn't around. It nullified memories and thoughts that served no practical purpose.

I learned how to drink at the boarding house and it was the best lesson of my life. I learned to savour each mouthful, each warm feeling in my gut and each overactive synapse soothed in my brain. I found a good level of drunkenness and tried to maintain it.

The drunk version of me was the first to get it. I had long nights feeling the warmth and safety of self-assurance resting over me.

To start with, the post-booze blues were hideous. I thought about the feel of Lanny's touch in the morning, and the yearning would get stronger as I sat next to the lake in the afternoon. Those feelings became unbearable at night if I couldn't drown my brain with wine.

I thought about how I'd fucked up, how she'd recoiled at something I'd said on the phone, how I'd tried to be more normal and then given the wrong impression. I thought about conversations and funnier lines for the future.

I thought constantly and my mind never rested until the booze reprogrammed my child-adult brain. The drink helped me stay awake and slow down the thoughts to only double-speed not ten-speed.

Still, there were too many nights without sleeping. A noisy, endless battle between the weak cunt versus the sociopath.

I'd sit at my window and watch outside. A big oak tree loomed outside with coils of ivy wrapped around it. It was a beautiful black shape outlined against the sky and swaying slightly in the wind.

I'd watch it be framed by the red and grey and purple of a sunrise. I'd trace the branches to the end, every one of them, a thousand tiny ends budding up.

Eventually I started to sleep, but then that became an addiction too. Twelve hours roving through my subconscious.

The nightmares were only life, distilled like absinthe...

15

ThudTHOOMthudTHOOMthudthudthudTHOOMthudTHOOMthudTHOOM.

I looked across at the seething mass. Up THUD down THOOM up THUD down THOOM left THUD right THOOM up THUD down THOOM. Some people were bopping exactly in time, some were out of time.

ThudthudTHOOMthudthudTHOOMthudthudTHOOMtha-thu-thu-THOOOM.

Heads jerked to the four beats per bar, legs tapped out time with an arm shake on the beat change. Thudthudtha-thu-thu-THOOOM. A sea of bodies flowed from one shit song into the next.

Lanny looked up, saw me, waved, pulled a wacky face and came over. She chugged back most of the four shots of sweet whiskey and coke I had in my right hand.

She looked into my face and smiled: "YOU OK THERE?" She ran her hand through my hair again and I wanted to be back at the bat hotel with her.

"YEAH, YEAH, GOOD THANKS." I was a fucking liar.

"WANNA DANCE?"

"YEAH, SURE, OK."

I downed the drink and lurched down into the mess of noise and bodies. I started matching the beat with the movement of my feet. It was all I did years later when I became a drummer.

Academic

Lanny grabbed my hands and flailed around, her hair flying like a beautiful tornado. I wished I could watch her in complete silence. I still wish I could now.

Lanny slid down and mimicked oral sex, her hands moving back and forward in time to the beat. I leaned back as if I was receiving a blowjob. People turned around and looked. Some of them clapped and laughed.

I needed more alcohol. I reached over, stroked her head, smiled, ands shouted: "DRINK" at Lanny. She smiled back then started dancing with the nearest person.

I ordered a triple shot, then I stood and watched her. She was blasting into the chaos, losing herself in it. I scanned around. I tried to understand it, but my warped brain started tuning it out. These people dancing in the silence in my head, slowing down, up THOOM down THUD up THOOM down THUD. Crazy, it's cr... fuck, let me concentrate.

A mass of semi-humans wailing, flirting, arguing, ready to excuse their shit the next day. Would they fuck the end-of-night arsehole, fight over a spilled beer, or finally tell the truth to someone they loved? It all rattled in their skulls and the booze released it all.

I daydreamed of nuclear bombs, melting flesh, abortion clinics on every corner catching these fuckers earlier. No, no, no. But then I was drawing out a tommy gun and mowing them down. Not one of them could die and the world feel the tiniest ripple. Fuck it, THUD fuck it THOOM, shit, concentrate.

Lanny came over and downed another half of my fresh booze. She kissed me and the taste of her lips was divine. She went cross-eyed and giggled at me.

She shouted: "YOU!"

I kissed her forehead and shouted: "YOU!"

She gripped around me, then she turned around as "Blame It On The Boogie" came on the vibrating speakers. She looked excited, then winked and smiled. She rushed back and joined in with the formation dance.

"Don't blame it on the sunshine..." Drink, fuck it, drink.

The hideous clichés of flirting were audible: "What's your favourite colour... What's your favourite animal... Hey, don't I know you?"

My heart sank at each of them, and yet I hated it when the person responded or flicked their finger.

Toilet time... I went to piss in a cubicle because I couldn't piss in front of others. Paper was floating in the yellow water, pebbledashed turds peeped out and the floor was wet with urine.

As I drained that night of drinking I could still hear the beat thudAHthoomAHthudOHHHthoomMmm.

As soon as I got out of there, I bumped into Erica and Rob.

"HI!" Rob screamed.

"ERICA?!"

"HEY!" She stuck out her tongue and looked at Rob. He was busy dancing on the spot.

I puckered up my lips.

Erica screamed: "YOU OK?!"

"AH, YOU KNOW," I shrugged.

Rob grinned: "JUST LOOK AS IF YOU'RE ENJOYING IT!"

I reeled slightly, shook my head and took a drink at that.

The music cut and people applauded. Relief passed over me, but my ears were buzzing and I felt dizzy.

Erica and Rob lingered and talked shit to each other. Erica giggled a lot. Rob had a broad grin on his face. Ah...

Lanny took her time in saying goodnight to old and new friends. She was a kind woman and was endlessly hugging people. By the time she made it over to me the place was almost empty.

She grabbed my hand and led me outside.

"Let's get a drink at yours, yeah?" she said.

"Yeah, Lan," I said as she pulled me along. "I need one."

She let out a big "DREEEEEE!" as she pushed her hand against my face: "You always need one!"

Next, there was fresh air and the sound of a gentle breeze. I looked up and there were bright stars against the moon.

I smiled dreamily and said: "It's a beautiful night."

Lanny poked me in the side and whispered: "Look."

Over to the right of us, ten yards away, was a guy hunched over a woman. I couldn't see her face but I could hear her moaning quietly. He was kneeling, arms down in the gravel. Back and forth, slowly, deliberately, his lily-white arse peeking out from where he'd tugged his jeans down.

His arms were dripping long, fascinating rivulets of blood.

"Come on," Lanny smiled and tugged at my hand again. "It's cold out here."

I looked back as we walked, and the guy kept fucking away and his blood kept flowing.

16

Lanny looked up at me with her long legs crossed over on the floor. Those wide-spaced eyes... she was always such a beauty. She smiled as she took a long swig from the bottle of Merlot.

Rob and Erica dry-humped through words before Erica started groping. Lanny and I talked through it and over it, with Erica chugging drink as Rob grew increasingly randy.

They left after twenty minutes. We heard the door shut, then some shuffles and "yes's..."

The walls hadn't got any thicker and Lanny laughed: "Hammer and tongs springs to mind!"

The mental image of them going at it was nauseating: "Hey! I haven't eaten yet!"

Then Lan said, with a dirty grin: "But you will soon."

We drank more, with idle chat and daft jokes, and Lanny was halfway down her bottle in another twenty minutes.

Then the realisation. Shit! I hadn't bought condoms. I'd tried to remember it earlier. I was a fucking IDIOT.

Lanny staggered up and sat next to me on the bed.

She said: "Sit on the floor between my legs."

She wrapped her legs around me. They filled her tight jeans... Oh, Lanny.

"Lemme practice head massage."

She kneaded my head and said: "You like?"

The sensation was incredibly soothing: "I love."

Lanny kissed the top of my head and said: "I know you do."

"They're quiet..." I said, and nodded towards the wall.

She continued to knead my head: "Yeah, they are..."

I said: "Thank-you."

She paused, then said: "I like this wine. You got a new one."

It wasn't new. She'd had it twice before. "Yeah."

She giggled: "I feel good!" She started kneading her bare foot against my groin. "You like?"

"I love."

I took a long swig, got up and looked up at her. The curve of her, even when she was sitting, was a marvel.

She leaned back, looked up at the ceiling and squeezed her tits together: "You love these more!" She peeled off her green, shiny top. Now there was just her dark red sports bra and a smile. She patted her pockets... "You got one?"

I looked in the drawer to make an act of it, knowing it was empty: "Shit... no..."

"I'll get one from Rob."

"You think they're done?"

"Yeah... yeah..." she got up, in her sports bra and jeans, and fumbled out the door. I watched her bubble-butt wiggle away. I leaned back and took off my shirt, enjoying the feel of the wine and the smell of Lanny. I was skinny and pale, but I felt like something special right there.

I heard a loud door-knock, then the door being swung open, then a pause, then Lanny's voice rising: "oh... my... GOD!"

I sprung up and darted out, fearing the worst. Violence, anything. Lanny was open-mouthed in the doorway. I peered around the corner, then Lanny yanked me next to her.

It was carnage.

I processed it. I remembered Erica's period...

Ah. Oh, oh, ah.

There were black sticky blobs on Rob's wall and black had smeared to red on his pressed white bedsheet. Further blobs were on the floor and on his chair. Rob had his stained lucky shirt in his hand. He must have been working at a blob on the wall with it. Erica was under the bloodied sheet on the bed. She was wide-eyed and shit-faced with an odd grin on her face.

I looked closer at Rob. He had poured water over himself but the red-black gloop was still in his hair. He must have finger-fucked Erica and got that shit over his head from wiping sweat away. He had turned a deathly shade of grey.

I started laughing hugely, widely and insanely.

Academic

"HAHAHAA-HAHAHAA…" I tried to draw breath and almost fell over. I started to feel my bladder tense and strain with it. "Huh-huhHAHAHAHA!"

They all silently looked at me.

A few more laughs belted out before I could control myself.

Lanny punched my arm, "YOU!" and then we set about helping to clean the room.

17

It didn't change straight away with Lanny. It was six weeks after that night, and we had warm sex and many laughs after it.

People forget anything by the next morning unless their attitude is against you. If their disposition changes then a hair in the sink or anything trivial can set them off. I can't imagine anything broke our relationship other than my oddness. Now I can see what was there was hardly carved in stone.

Lanny spent another month away for her physiotherapy training. I became ever more introverted and strange.

Lanny eased the matter into a conversation as we half-watched fucking *Friends*: "I've met a guy." She took a drink and her smile was soft, with no sense of victory or hurt.

"Oh yeah?" I drank some more. I wasn't surprised, although I lurched inside. I had imagined this moment and tried to steel myself towards it.

"Yeah, he's cool. He reminds me of you sometimes," she said. "I think you'll like him."

"Oh yeah?" The nausea grew a little, but that could be controlled too.

I poured another glass of wine for Lanny.

It was night-time and the bats started chittering.

"They're still here?!" she looked up and then glared at me. "Can't you get rid of them?"

I shrugged: "They're an endangered species."

"How humane," she laughed. "Bet you don't even squish spiders..."

We drank for a while before she left.

She hugged me and said she'd get in touch soon.

That turned into a couple of weeks.

"Steve..." she eventually phoned me at the boarding-house. "Can I come and see you tomorrow?"

How does anyone respond to that? Even her plummy voice made me smile...

My heart leaped and I finally slept one of my 12 hour sleeps for the first time in a fortnight.

18

Now if anyone says someone is like me, I crack up laughing. I was a fucking child back then so I could believe it more.

I figured her latest boyfriend was just a better looking version of me... minus the neuroses but with a smaller cock.

I had felt lost, crazy and alone. I didn't go to teacher training and they didn't miss me. I emailed the essays that I could easily chug out in a few hours.

As for life, no amount of masturbation or booze helped. I told myself no other woman would want me. I hardly slept and I felt ill when I ate. I wallowed in misery like a long and skinny pig.

Lanny didn't see any of it as she blasted in. My sunken eyes, my shaking hands. Just that smile again, and her beautiful brown skin warming the world around her.

"'ELLO YOU!"

"Hey, Lanny."

Then she softly and quickly hugged me: "Cheer up!"

That did make me happy: "Alright..."

I had saved a good bottle of red wine for her. She giggled and suddenly I felt both better and lost again.

We drank the wine and shared yet more bad jokes.

Lanny asked: "What's red and pink and can't turn around in a corridor?"

I thought, and then said: "I dunno."

"A baby with a javelin in its head! Dreeeeeeee...!"

My eyes bugged out: "Well, that turned fucking dark..."

"Dreeee..." and now she was dancing with her buttocks on the floor. "More wine, please!"

After a while, the booze continued to loosen her tongue enough that she got onto Stuart: "He like, well... he sorta whips it out before he cums." Lanny pouted: "He cums in my hair or on my face, and sometimes in my eyes!"

Oh no. Now I had been ushered into the role of confidante.

I said: "That's just wrong." It appalled me how people can turn anything into a power game.

"And, you know, I mean *don't tell anyone*," and she poked my arm, "but I was on the loo the other day and he – well – *he tried to climb over the door*! Dreeeeeee..."

"What?"

"I shouted 'WHAT ARE YOU DOING?' and he got down," Lanny pursed her lips: "Then he said he wanted to see me poo. And, get this..." She took a long drink. "He asked me if he could lay under my glass table and watch me poop on top of it!"

I was stunned. I wanted to scream at her, but the best I could manage was: "And you're still with him?"

"Well, you know," she smiled, "he's a character."

A CHARACTER! Hollywood screenwriters couldn't write this shit spewing from her.

We polished off a couple of bottles of wine until Lanny left at 10pm.

She said: "I have to get home."

"You sure?"

"I'm sure that I'm sure," and Lanny pecked my cheek.

It infuriated and confused me.

Was she going back to take another eyeful of cum?

19

Eventually the lack of sex helped. When you stop holding someone and feeling their naked flesh, all of the inanity slides into focus. I had no doubt Lanny was feeling the same about me too.

The next time I saw Lanny she started talking about Stuart again: "I had his precious little puddle of cum in my bellybutton and he licked it up and then he kissed me!" She held her tongue out of her mouth and started to "Dreeeeee..."

I was boozed up and in the mood for telling the truth: "Why do you put up with that stuff?"

Lanny stopped laughing: "Huh?" Then she paused before saying: "Um." Then another pause before: "My sister's prettier."

"What?" She'd never mentioned a sister to me...

She pulled out a picture from her tight jeans. She must have carried it around with her.

Academic

She handed me the photo. Her parents were an attractive pale woman and a handsome black man. Below them, in some cheesy portrait against a photographer's white background, were two Lannys. Different clothes but the same body, the same smile, the same eyes. They must have been 19 or 20 at the time. The copied Lannys were both beautiful.

I stared. Had I gone crazy? "But... she's your... twin."

"I know that, you twonk, but Vicky's so much prettier than me..." Lanny said, pointing to one of the Lannys on the photo. "*Look properly*. Dad's always said it and I know Mum feels it."

I studied the photo like a frame from a beautiful film: "I'm sorry, Lan, I didn't even know that wasn't you."

"Oh, you just don't understand," she sniffed.

I apologised and offered her another drink, but more thoughts were bubbling away.

This fucking NOISE people surround themselves in. Beauty tips, loud shitpop, celebrity gossip, dire TV, lousy books. The more stupid the better, as long as they forced out thoughts and filled them with accepted wisdom.

It poisoned people, but I loved Lanny and wrestled with the truth... Why couldn't I be more like her?

I clamped my lips together and kept my feelings inside. It was an artform that I would perfect over the rest of my life.

20

The lessons of life repulsed me. Wasn't true love about softening of the blows of life?

My fiancee, years later, wanted me to shake the hand of the mouth-breather cop she had chosen to dump me for. She wrote: *"I want you to be friends and just accept things."*

Fuck that. And, of course, my supposedly new friend ended up threatening to kill me. But, hey, more on that later...

Back in the late 90's, Lanny called one day with much the same deal. A few pleasantries then: "I'm having a party with everyone... I'm..." and I heard her exhale, "moving away. To the hospital in Wycombe," she said. "For good."

I didn't hear much of the rest of what Lanny said, other than when she brightened and said: "Stuart's coming. You guys can meet up!"

I said, flatly: "Ok. I'm ready."

I wrote down Lanny's address. Unsurprisingly it was in a swanky area near to the university. The party was two nights away and I slept perhaps an hour over that time.

I filled the day drinking red wine, and got to her place around 7pm. It was Victorian, redbrick, lavish and with an imposing door.

I knocked and Erica answered it. She made a habit of popping up in my life when I least expected it. She grinned and said: "Well, howdy there!"

"I have drink..." I smiled and trembled. I could hear plenty of people and I saw a hall with high ceilings behind her. "Two bottles," I said, holding them up awkwardly.

The place was huge. Ceiling roses, picture rails, covings, oak floors and a giant widescreen TV. I found out Lanny shared it with three other medical workers. They were all female and none of them were as attractive as her. The nurse fetish is infantile – your odds are as good or bad as everywhere else...

There were cards and presents. Lanny was bubbling around in the kitchen mixing punch. I handed her the two bottles.

"Hey, you! Thanks..." she gave me the torso hug where the woman keeps her lower body separate. No, no, no. Now she had the fear that getting her groin against my cock was repulsive, even through layer after layer of clothing.

Stuart was standing next to her. He was good looking, tall, and slightly grey skinned. "This is Stuart," she said.

"Hello, Stephen," he said. His posh accent was the only distinguishing thing about him. He was a forerunner of Christian Grey and a progeny of Harry Flashman. What was it about middle-upper class women that made them attracted to sadistic pricks?

Lanny asked: "You want a drink?"

"Always."

At least she smiled at that.

Stuart's personality was dull. There is no value in recording the enunciated, upper-class shit that dribbled from his mouth. It left with me was a strong feeling that Lanny had considered me her "bit of rough."

Stuart mostly stood quietly next to Lanny while she yakked to her friends. He was dull to the point that I couldn't imagine him having sex, let alone spraying cum like a human sprinkler.

There was bad music, including bland reggae. There was also much laughing and small talk. Her friends gave me a wide berth as I sat on a comfy leather seat. I drank a lot but tried to look as if I wasn't. I mixed 80% vodka with lemonade and made sure people didn't see me pour. Then I would try to tune out existence.

Over the noise and the dizziness growing in my head, one voice kept breaking in. That horrible drawl of a *camp man*.

I know homosexuality is a wonderful thing. Frankly, people should be encouraged to buttfuck and eat pussy to help overpopulation. They are the heroes of humanity and I wish I had been born gay.

Sadly, I couldn't get over my addiction to the curves of women and I couldn't get over my hatred of the camp man. The voice, the fashion and the interior design all added up to yet another vacuous cliché. Like the hideous alpha hetero-male, he is a vicious mix of fakeness, power games and bullshit ideologies.

I could hear him from a distance, even over the drone of Erica's endless yakking.

Academic

His Scandinavian vibrato voice cut through the air: "SWEETIE, just look at your HAIR... Why are you wearing THAT with YOUR derriere..." This ghastly stereotype made me want to vomit. Why do people let their sexuality place them into another ridiculous club? This desire to fit in, to behave. Why do people believe it? "Isn't it just DARLING... Oh, look at YOU!!!"

A gang of gay groupies were giggling at his judgments. He was never short of people around him, including Lanny. She broke into her raking "DREEEEEEE!" pre-laughs at his catty comments. Stuart stood nearby with an aloof smile. Maybe he was plotting the course of his next salty missile?

I made the mistake of going up to get some booze when the camp man was nearby. "Oh, I've heard all about YOU," he said, and giggled. He was short, blonde and attractive. He had ruddy cheeks and a fixed sneer.

I said: "Oh yeah?" I felt the dizziness rage more. "Want a drink?" I poured out some of Lanny's limp punch.

"I don't DRINK!" He waved a hand: "It poisons your body!"

"Fair enough." As I walked off I heard him whisper deliberately loud enough for me to hear: "Look at those clothes..."

One of Lanny's housemates, a tall thirty-something pear-shaped blonde, failed to stifle a giggle.

I flipped: "What did you say?"

"Oh, nothing," Campboy said, and he shuffled back a little.

"WHAT?!" I shouted and started shaking. The place went silent immediately.

"I didn't say anything," he whined.

"Yeah, you did," I hissed, "you CUNT."

"I didn't say anything!" Now his voice was something like a wail... the typical retreat of the sarcastic idiot.

I felt Lanny's hand on my shoulder, "Calm down," but her smile was awkward and false, "Steve, calm down, ok?"

My brain did settle but the thing that spurted out was: "NO. FUCKING NO."

I went towards him to scream more, but people were pulling me back. Stuart was one of them.

Cuntboy liked that: "What's wrong with HIM?"

"It's just the drink," Lanny said. Ah, ah, ah...

I flew again, directing it at him because he was there: "It's not the FUCKING DRINK! This is ME! Maybe this CUNT should drink. It might make him more FUCKING HUMAN!"

They pulled me outside the front door. It wasn't violent, I was just led away. Some of them even said "bye" and smiled at me before they scooted back in.

I sat on the stoop of Lanny's giant building and rubbed my stupid head. Lanny came out and sat next to me: "You ok?" she said, with more care than I'd ever heard from her. She ran her fingers through my hair for the last time and said: "Oh, Steve..."

"Yeah," I was still shaking. "I'm fine."

"I better go," she said and smiled. She kissed my nose.

I fumbled for something: "Good luck, ok? With everything."

"I'll write, ok?" she said and smiled again. We both got up and she gave me another torso hug and then pushed back as she said: "Take good care. Always, ok?"

"I will. And you too."

I started to walk off and looked back. She was already halfway through the door.

Then, as in the increasingly long sleeps, that little voice was talking to me again as I walked back to the boarding house.

I tried to beat down those strange voices that reverberated in my head, but this time they didn't stop. They even *smiled* as the little voice said "Good," and I liked it.

21

Lanny did write, and so did Brad. I'll never know why.

I got letters and emails from Lanny every few months for five years. I wrote back with funny stories that I thought might make her laugh. Her smile was indelibly fixed in my mind, and I remain crushed I never saw her in the flesh again.

Stuart cheated on Lanny after a year. She moved on to a Swedish guy called Morten. As I became immersed in my so-called career, she would tell me how wonderful he was. Ah well...

Morten and Lanny set out to travel around the world. After three months he dumped her in Australia and she had to work to get herself back home. The last I heard was that.

Her last email was almost a plea for help. I should have flown out there, but I was foolishly lost in the world of teaching.

Brad married Cassie. He became a website designer and wrote terrible poems on married life and the tedious cosiness of toothpaste pushed from the middle. After four years, they divorced and he went crazy. The last I heard was that.

Brad didn't matter to me. Men were largely meaningless because they were as dim as I was. But I kept thinking about Lanny and the prospect of new, fascinating women.

Why did they make me laugh so much more than men? It was beyond attraction, it was intimacy and emotional truth.

So, inevitably, what followed was Deanna interspersed with the almost equal stupidity of being a teacher.

Oh, just stab me in the forehead and save me the hassle of donkey-kicking my ballsack...

22

When I was 20, I had completed a computer survey. It gave me a list of 31 suitable jobs. I was still working bar and finishing my Film degree.

Academic

The first of the jobs flagged up by the computer was "secretary." I was lousy at small talk and was often inadvertently offensive. Drunks love a sleazy line, but mainstream employers hate them.

I scanned downward and somewhere in the low-teens of prospective careers was "teacher." Completing the course proved to be easy, but living the life would be much different.

I considered various jobs which were self-reliant. *Writer?* I wasn't mainstream enough. *Journalist?* I'd have to write about politicised bullshit. *Male prostitute?* Ah, too nervous.

I realised teaching was the best fit, despite my hatred of High School. My school's atmosphere had been one of impending violence that clearly drove teachers to the brink of insanity...

I had a German teacher who would sob loudly in his cupboard after we did badly in a vocabulary quiz. The poor bloke was surrounded by a horde of psychotic students... one of which kneed me in my left eye during a cross country run.

That knee permanently fucked up my vision in the eye but also clonked a little thought into my head. It forced out some the sarcastic indifference I'd built up around myself.

Luckily, my Sixth Form College had felt very different. It gave teachers a small chance to weed out the assholes. It was non-compulsory and students could pick the subjects they wanted to do. For all its flaws and frustrations, it was a more relaxed atmosphere and a definite improvement from my dictatorial school.

Academic

Straight after my Film and English degree ended, I went back to the college I had attended three years before.

Back when I was a student, the college only had a few hundred students. Many of the teachers were eccentrics. They were from the days before "Curriculum 2000," which was an eerie Big Brother concept that fixated on homogenising students.

My favourite of three lovely college teachers was Mr. Greene. He was my History teacher. He was an unassuming bearded guy touching sixty who looked after his recently disabled wife. He would tell us largely untold – yet true – tales of how the 1905 Russian Revolution failed because Lenin's train into Moscow was late. Then, with a certain glint in his eye, he told us how Napoleon lost at Waterloo because he had piles and couldn't ride into battle. He was a quiet man with a love of history who had found his inner storyteller.

Although it seemed at odds with my personality, guided by my old Media teacher I gradually learned to love teaching lessons. I mixed teaching for a day a week with my studies, and what followed was nuts... I taught Film/English/Media for exactly one day short of twenty years. I was forty when I quit.

A huge part of my life involved ranting about great movies, trying out various real-life stories, and helping students understand – and hopefully enjoy – worthwhile films.

I always had "Imposter Syndrome." I had fluked into teaching – mostly through my mentor quitting to write Roman adventure novels. I was the youngest teacher and was voluntarily thrown into a confusing world that took me years to figure out.

What I learned was the only problem with academia was *teachers*. I was around them for all those years, and it's embarrassing to refer to myself as one of them.

I taught for a long time but please don't call me a teacher...

23

I come from a working-middle class background. I grew up on a housing estate, but it was a plush one where people mostly owned their own houses.

One of my friends was called "Stanley" because he carried a Stanley Knife with him at all times. He would occasionally flash it as his deadly and pee-wee warning to a scared world. Years later, he ended up serving a few years for GBH.

In terms of family, my father was the accountant for a company that supplied arcade games, jukeboxes and fruit machines. Before she got sick, my mother was a hairdresser and then a housewife.

When I started teaching, it was obvious I didn't talk in a similar way to other teachers. I have a local accent and I swear more than is acceptable. I also have a base sense of humour, but fart and sex jokes don't truly demean like sarcasm does. That's why I banned it in my lessons.

Academic

My fellow teachers' main strategy to control a class was to be a bigger arsehole than the students. They responded to problems through snide insults, wordplay and sarcasm rather than direct comments: "Why don't you come up here and teach," a hipster dickhead had sneered, "because I'm *sure* you could do a better job than me..." The lady teacher with a handbag shaped like a teapot would say: "Well, I suppose if you didn't understand *anything* you'd think that might be correct."

My first role was teaching GCSE Media to students who had failed at school. That class included Jonjo, who was a 19 year-old (just two years younger than me) and a hulking 6'4" presence. He told me that he was an "internet pioneer." He would video himself and his gal-pal fucking on a webcam, then sell passwords to look at the footage. For a guy who had failed a lot of courses, Jonjo certainly knew his way around a computer.

That time was before DVDs, and I'd laboriously spend hours setting up VCR clips the night before.

Halfway through my tenth lesson, I felt a familiar gurgle in my stomach that meant I needed to shit. Irritable Bowel Syndrome. It seemed like I was collecting syndromes.

I made my apologies, squirted in the toilet, then returned. I popped in the next videotape and it was a porno of a cock entering an arsehole in extreme close-up. Then a gob of spit dribbled into the black cave before ol' dick probed back in. I have an aversion to anal sex, and the whole thing set me back on my heels.

Academic

The class erupted into laughter.

Jonjo laughed wildly: "Yer getcha tapes mixed up?"

It's times like that when you live or die. Most teachers flip out and, by doing so, they signal their prissiness. Respectable folks blush and deal with it as methodically as they can. Unfortunately, that just sets themselves up for more pranks.

The trick is to go further. You can't do that in High School, but you can at college. You can't get fired for cursing. For all their boundary pushing, students have limits too.

"That's not me," I said. "My cock is WAY bigger."

I then went on to say how the woman looked bored. I described how to tell if a woman has had an orgasm. The six previously disaffected students were interested in the nipples hardening and the boobs puffing out before sagging at the moment of orgasm.

Hopefully the guys treated their gals better after that, but it was yet another time where they laughed then looked startled.

I looked over to my left and there – steaming from her ears in the doorway – was Mrs. McKay. "WHAT ARE YOU TALKING ABOUT!? WHAT IS THIS DISGUSTING TALK!?"

She was 50-year-old Lutheran and English Literature teacher from the classroom next-door.

"WHERE IS YOUR TUTOR?"

The group now stopped wincing and laughed again.

"Hello," I smiled at her, "I'm the new teacher."

She glared at me: "I'M REPORTING THIS!" And, with that, she stormed off.

I never copped any flak, but I did start to talk more quietly.

I quickly learned that teachers were almost exclusively smug, phony left-wing, backstabbing, pseudo-intellectual, frequently stupid, hypocritical cunts.

Deanna eventually conditioned me to fully deal with that.

Sadly, back then I was still an overgrown child and love was something that could screw me in the arse without lube.

24

I was formally hired when I was twenty-two. I had been observing then teaching part-time at the college for a year before that. Young teachers were *always* given the worst classes, a form of hazing as an initiation into that middle class world.

My blank, unemotional face helped. My experience of life meant that I could easily feign being at ease in any situation. That happened when I was wandering down the corridor after a lesson, and Frances Wilson said: "Hello, Steve!"

I said: "Hello?" I felt like I had seen him before but I rummaged around in my memory and found nothing.

I decided Wilson was a semi-retarded administrator who needed a little chat. I smiled and nodded encouragingly.

Academic

He had large bottle-top glasses, slicked grey hair and an eerie fixed smile. He looked like a bad guy from an Italian Giallo movie. He asked: "So, how is the teaching progressing?"

I said: "I like it. It's fun."

"And you're getting along with your GCSE students?"

This was weirdly specific: "They're a handful," then I smiled and said, "but I've got giant hands." I held them up proudly.

"Good for your cricket, old chap?" Had this guy been researching me online? "I understand you're quite the bowler."

I shifted uncomfortably in my low seat, but then grinned: "My reputation precedes me!"

"I used to be quite the batsman in my day..."

This was bizarre but, hey-ho, what wasn't... "Any luck?"

"These old eyes," he pointed at his glasses. "One needed 20/20 vision to rack up the centuries, I'm afraid."

Was this myopic crustie trying to chat me up? I said: "You could always squint," and I drew my mouth to one side.

Wilson laughed and said: "Well, I'm glad to tell you we're offering you a full-time contract."

"What?"

He reached out his tiny hand and shook mine: "I'm the new Principal and we're sorting out staffing for next year."

I stared forwards, as confused as ever.

Academic

25

I discovered teaching Film was the skill of expressing beautiful hidden meanings that possibly never existed. This had been done for centuries over shit like Shakespeare, so why not for films I loved? Existentialist angst in *Barfly*, ideological shock in *Dawn of the Dead,* new-wave French paranoia in *The 400 Blows*, post-war malaise in *The Third Man* and *Taxi Driver* and so on...

I delivered all that with enough passion that the students and examiners believed it. I also believed it daily for each seven-hour gig. By 4pm I didn't want to speak any more. I poured everything into teaching and little was left afterward.

The teacher was me, but a condensed me. A ball of energy, tirades, and anecdotes. Words, words, words. Sometimes without thought, just the moment pounding on.

It worked. The students came to the lessons, they enjoyed the course, they got the top grades and I felt that simple joy of being helpful.

Throughout the first three years, Wilson mostly let me be. My students never ratted me out on my coarse language and strange stories about my life. All they cared about was their grades, and that was all I cared about too.

I was content as far down the food chain as I could be, then one of my 23 superiors persuaded me to re-apply for Head of Department. It was a childish token title where I'd get paid more for the exact same tasks.

Academic

With increasing student numbers, the college needed to hire another teacher and establish the role of Head of Media. I now had experience, the top student grades, qualifications, and high scores at their precious inspections. I also hated paperwork...

An angular giant named Lenny got it. He had very little teaching experience, little training and average results... Ah, Wilson, *that* Lenny. Lenny who went to the right evening soirees and the right lunchtime gatherings. He licked the correct hole in the correct way at the correct time.

But, hey, Lenny was a real team player until he ended up fucking a 16-year-old student. More importantly, he didn't know to use editing software, he barely knew how to operate a camera, and his students complained about how lazy his lessons were.

Like any job, teaching forced you into complicity and caring about drivel. I cared, but I didn't care enough. I was a quiet well-behaved outsider, but I was awful at small talk and bad at kissing ass. I was scrupulously polite to the other teachers, but I avoided them as much as possible. I had enough of them in meetings and conversations that were impossible to escape from.

The older teachers had affected ways of talking and an unconscious way of talking to me like a child. Many were pale-looking zombies, while others who used to have fire in their bellies were left with a tiny nervous tic... a laugh after every sentence, a "mmm" mumble, a twitching eye, a jerking neck.

Meanwhile, the younger teachers were frantically trying to please superiors and make it to the next fix of caffeine, nicotine or a Friday night-out. Their pleasures were getting smaller and smaller as "career" became interchangeable with "life" for them.

Most weren't bad people, but they were in love with the money they earned for being as half-arsed as possible. They'd die slowly for the promise of a holiday in Portugal, a new car, a bigger house, the removal of risk and the acceptance of nothing.

I didn't feel anything towards them whatsoever. I was merely scared I'd be worn into one of them by each tiny blow.

26

A few months into my fourth year of teaching it started getting to me. I was 25 years old, and surrounded by teachers with comfortable houses and comfortable families and comfortable lies.

It was compulsory to observe three lessons a year and all I saw was mundane, passionless shit. I would have preferred to gouge my eyes out than suffer two years of a shit-for-brains nervously whining about Psychology or English Literature. The higher up the ladder they climbed, the more boring shit they spouted.

Naturally I was polite but naturally they started to mistrust my detachment.

I remember the College's Open Day before I quit for the first time. High School students would come and look at leaflets selling the courses. They would travel in giggling packs, flitting from one room to the next, grabbing a leaflet then surging out.

Management looked upon the day as hugely important. That was another self-important lie. The truth was students would decide where to study through abstract reasons such as friends, location or vague ideas of a college's reputation.

The building was a shithole and the teachers looked moronic, yet the students still went there. A fucking leaflet wasn't going to change their mind.

I'd agreed to set up a room for Film Studies, but I got to my room at 9am and fell asleep on the desk. I was going through shit at home with my sick mother and I'd been staying up late to talk to an American-Irish gal I'd met in a bar. Those are whiny excuses in retrospect, but they're all I have. I always taught well, but I promoted myself and the college badly.

That Irish gal seemed something wonderful, interested in the same things and also in the same profession. She was a teaching assistant in the nearby school for handicapped students.

Sleep wasn't coming easily or regularly, and when The Head of Art stormed in at 10am she had did have a point, albeit a dull one. Yolanda screamed: "WHAT ARE YOU FUCKING DOING?"

I bolted upright: "Sorry, I must have drifted off."

"You said you were going to set up the room." She was very pretty and I didn't know whether that had condensed into arrogance. "WHAT ABOUT THE ROOM?!"

"Sorry," I said, "I figured it was a waste of time."

"But what about TEXTILES?"

"Sorry?" She had tiny hairs protruding from her nostrils.

"I could have used that room for TEXTILES."

"Sorry, I thought there were other rooms."

"But that one is better than the others!"

"Oh..." There seemed nothing else to say.

"Is something wrong with you or...?" She didn't give a shit one way or another, but her scowl softened. "You can talk to me..."

She placed her hand on my arm and I jerked back. I hated to be touched. Most of the time, your skin is all you have.

"No, look... I'm fine," I said. "I'm just tired... alright?"

"Pah!" Then she launched into 100 words of machine-gun words that I forgot within an hour of hearing them.

Yolanda stormed out, and I watched the door easing back on the safety catch where she had tried to slam it and failed.

I let my head sink back down on the desk, and hoped another crazy dream about Lanny would fill it.

27

Wilson remained atop our retarded teaching gene pool.

He had ridden the slippery pole of promotion and cum-guzzled superior's bullshit to get there.

Academic

I should have expected what followed. The troubles at home worsened further and I would occasionally turn up two minutes late for the five minute meeting he gave at the start of every day.

He called me over at the end of one and put his furtive brain and animatronic face into overdrive: "I really don't like the fact you come to *every* meeting late." Scrunch up eyes, Wilson...

"Sorry, I have..." In four years not one meeting had any useful information that I couldn't get easily that same day.

"Ensure you make an effort to come on time *every* day." Open eyes, look nonchalant, Wilson... "It's an important part of the college's function."

"I always ask someone if..." It was just a way for him to be Caesar to his masses, an opportunity to cough and hush the room.

"*Every* day please, and thanks." Grin, grin, Wilson...

He was suddenly in my world and fingernails in my brain. He was no worse than other bosses... he was just HERE.

His grey eyes didn't blink enough. His plastic hair and the tiny suits he wore. The way he squinted when he fake smiled at me. His satisfied laugh, the noise it made in his throat. The smell of coffee and shit on his breath.

In meetings I started having maniacal fantasies of screaming at him. I would think of him sobbing, or naked, or the change in his face after a fist had slammed into it.

Academic

I hated how he made me sit at a desk on Parents' Evening when no-one was there: "Well, pretend you're working, old chap."

He moved my room four years in a row for "strategic reasons." Then there were Wilson's endless speeches about money and grants... his personal parking space nearest to the entrance... the way he strolled in at any point if he needed you, while *you* needed an appointment to see him... the way he greeted everyone with a "how are you?" and never waited for an answer.

This cunt enjoyed the fact I sometimes turned up pale and shaking. He enjoyed ruling the damaged.

The more I was messed up, the more it justified Wilson and his position of authority over me. I foolishly imagined him in some ivory tower, lording it over the peasants around him.

I didn't want his power, I just didn't want him to have it.

In fact, I didn't want anyone to have it... until I stupidly broke my independence by giving it to a woman.

28

I had met Deanna in my local pub. The twang of her American accent caught my attention: "I'd like more a-that, pleez." She was drinking Guinness, a testament to her roots...

I said: "Hello."

Her glossy pink lips were a little rubbed out on the three pint glasses in front of her: "Hey... YOU... I like your shirt..."

"Miami Dolphins."

"It's very GREEEEEN."

"I like your top too."

"All of it?" She was wearing a black diaphanous top, and she lent back on the barstool.

"Yeah."

Her large blue eyes bulged: "Ya know ah'm from New York?"

"It's not hard to guess..." I paused and waited.

"Ah'm Deanna O'Connor."

"That almost rhymes..."

She smiled, shut them opened her eyes again, trying to refocus. "An' you are?"

I said in my usual monotone: "I am Steve."

"Whadda you do?"

"I try to teach."

She purred back: "Y'know ah teach inna school over there," and she poked a finger towards the local school for students with disabilities. "Ah'm an assistant."

My next line was another shitty one: "Want to assist me?"

As she did for the next eighteen months, Deanna grinned with her lips closed.

Her growling "Hmmmm..." was like a grizzly bear going in for the kill. "Ah think ah'd like that..."

I loved the way Deanna stared at me as we continued to talk. There was no artifice and no coyness. It was very un-English... pure filth and all the more wonderful because of it.

That night – and further nights – developed exactly how you would imagine.

As we talked before her return to the States, we found out we both wrote, read similar books, liked the same movies and TV.

We talked about writing and we hit on something – she was a huge fan of Kerouac, not so far from the guys I loved. What clinched it was that she'd read a story of mine on a website. I have unnatural friendship towards people that like my work. I gave her some new names by equally great, but lesser known, writers. Later I gave her some of those books and more of my work. She devoured them, and started writing more herself.

We also liked to talk dirty and Deanna's clit would get hard. She couldn't stop stroking it and I couldn't stop lapping at it.

29

Deanna lived in Long Island. Even online, the intensity of those first meetings grew so quickly that I was aware of the speed but I couldn't slow down.

We found a way to talk for hours every night: AOL Instant Messenger, e-mails, phone calls. We sent each other stories and poems.

Academic

We seemed to be trying to outduel each other when it came to clichés. She wrote:

I've been wasting time
Here on Earth
Writing with nothing to show
Drinking with nothing to drink about
Fucking just to fuck
Smoking just to make
Things clear enough
Bitching just to bitch
And dying just to live….
I'll wait for your
love till I am old and grey
Till the sun refuses to shine anymore
and Dreams stop being
just what they are
I'll talk my mouth dry
of how I loved you
all awhile this earth
was churning against
me and nothing could
hold me back from the
love you bring
I'll wait till My fingers
are curled up like prunes

Till I write the last I love you
Your heart matches mine
and in this Dream we win
and nothing else fails
And I'll still always see you
smiling against my face
and your eyes will hold
more beauty than heaven even knows
And I'll remember all the lines and verses
and how you bleed for me and How I did the same
in this universe we are no further
apart than any shining star
I still look up at you every nite...

Nothing like love to make simpletons out of anyone, huh?

30

After another week Deanna signed letters and emails as *Yr Irish Lass*. I had fallen hook, line and sinker.

She woke me up from the stupor of Lanny and my teaching job. I also wrote more because now I had someone to write for.

But after this initial blast, Deanna disappeared for a week. No screen-name and no answers. I didn't have her home address, which should have rung alarm bells, but ah, ah...

I went through a finding agency. It gave me three addresses with her name... I wrote to each one.

Within a week, Deanna emailed to say she had cried when she got the letter. She said that she thought of me constantly and that she needed me. She was just scared of "true love."

Three days later, she told me she had lied. She had a boyfriend. He was called Jay and she'd been with him for two years. It was from before her work experience in the UK and continued after she returned to the States.

I cried and I couldn't control it. Over the phone, Deanna screamed that she loved me and shouted: "I NEED TO BE A FUCKEN HERMIT. I SHOULD JUST LIVE ALONE AND WRITE."

Through my dumbass tears I said: "Well, it's a theory..."

Then she laughed, and I laughed too.

"Ya know I've been kinda slutty."

"That doesn't matter."

"I'm scared of fucken everythin'."

I resisted saying the line back I had to that. Instead I said: "Like what?"

"Like crowds 'n' big spaces... like anything unfamiliar."

"That stuff is fine, Dee."

"I fucken hate myself," Deanna said, "an' I can't change."

"It's your life..."

She spelled out the next line: "I, A, M, S, C, A, R, E,D..."

So it went on for another month or so. She stayed with him and worked with him, but refused to live with him.

In yet more conversations, Deanna said she barely talked to Jay. She told me that every time they had sex, it was angry and violent – like they hated each other.

Were these lies? You can only judge someone by what they say and do, but if you can't *see* what anyone does, you're blinded by words.

With the benefit of hindsight, I can see we were both trapped by our past relationships. Deanna was paranoid I'd find someone else and I was paranoid she would get tired of me.

My teaching job became eight hours of waiting to find ways to talk to Deanna again. I still planned the lessons, marked the essays, but Deanna rumbled away in my conscious thoughts.

She wrote: *"I am going to run away from the bad and to the good now, no matter what."* The email went on with: *"You are beautiful and so kind,"* and that I was her *"better half."*

Christmas came and Deanna said a prayer for me at Midnight Mass. I sent her dumb British gifts she had asked to try - hobnobs, creme eggs, mustard, marmite, and CDs. She said the hobnobs were "delicious," marmite was "icky," and that she'd played the CDs over and over.

Deanna sent another perfumed letter: *"We feel and breathe things the same way... I will never let you go, I <u>promise</u> you, you will always have my warmth and my words. You get me more than anyone has. You know what lurks beneath my soul and I'm not afraid to show you. I trust you and with that I love you!"*

I then wrote I'd never leave until Deanna told me to "fuck off." Then Seeing her words written in her oh-so-neat handwriting: *"A part of me will never be complete till we are together,"* made me utterly and stupidly in love.

I sent a student video from work where I had played a blind hitman. It was a mish-mash of *Ghost Dog* and *Zatoichi*.

Deanna told me she would masturbate to it, and that she thought of my cock shooting inside her. She sent me pictures of her tits and her pussy, and I sent her some of my cock.

It was nice... The teacher in me liked visual aids.

31

Back in Long Island, Deanna now worked in another school for men with disabilities. They had Down's Syndrome, severe ADHD or brain damage. Some were affectionate – like a 40-year-old called Old Man Jim – but most were mean-spirited and violent.

A kid named Robbie was the worst. He decided to take a bite out of Deanna's tit one day. The security guard had to pull Robbie's jaws apart to separate him. The guard was an ex-boyfriend and she hated needing his help.

Deanna called and said: "Old Man Jim is stealing again..."

"For the candy machines?"

"Yeah..." She paused and then rattled out: "He's such a sweetie, but he got a fucken erection when he hugged me today."

Academic

I couldn't help but laugh: "A man with taste!"

She shouted: "STOP IT!" but then she laughed too.

Neither Jim or the other kids learned anything – even with one teacher for every two kids. They'd been put there by parents who wanted rid of them but needed to feel ok about it.

I got swept in Deanna, despite sensing problems to start with. She was even more insecure than me and she would cry all too often. Somehow that fed into it all. I could wrap my arms around her and she'd look doe-eyed and everything would be sunshine and roses.

Everything great is magnified a hundred times by freshness... a seemingly endless enthusiasm that fuels any relationship in its infancy.

Deanna told me she'd loved threesomes in her early twenties and fucked her way through two years of college before she quit. She liked sadomasochistic porn and said she'd mimic what the stars did to each other. I liked smiling faces instead...

My fuck-up was taking the good things too lightly and letting the shit slide too easily. The screams to get her own way, the silences, the nymphomania, the increasingly violent emails she would write and then excuse the next day because she was drunk.

Conflict has a childlike element to it... deluded hope and talking people around. My truth was more basic. Every time she told me she loved me, all the shit transformed into chocolate ice cream. I always thought love was her way of rewriting her past.

Early on, she wrote a great deal about her monstrous father. He punished Deanna by making her hold books up in the rain like a female 12-year-old Jesus. I could understand why she thought all men were arseholes because they mostly were.

Her horrifically violent Catholic upbringing accounted for her being anti-abortion. I gave up arguing against her pro-life views after she wrote: *"As soon as there's something inside me, I'll know it, I'll feel life." S*o we started talking about having kids...

32

Deanna raised the idea of marriage. I find marriage an arbitrary concept – trust is kept with or without rules – and I regret not telling her so. But I let myself drop into it without complaint.

All of the time, Deanna was still off and on with Jay. In some moments, I felt sorry for the poor bastard. He was going to be crushed when Deanna finally ended up with me.

Nails were driven in that coffin when Deanna thought Jay was cheating on her. She raged through countless emails, even though she said she didn't want to be with him anymore.

She wrote: *"I am a shit... a fuck for feeling the way I do about Jay and I."* I told her otherwise... that I saw something beautiful inside her.

Academic

Jay bought her an expensive stereo, and I told her: "It makes me feel ill every time you're with him." I knew it was moronic, yet she replied with: "I love YOU!!!!!!!!!"

Deanna then started signing all of her letters and emails as: *"Yr future wife."* After a few of those, I signed mine: "Yr future husband."

I looked for places we could live together. It had to be near teaching jobs where Deanna could continue her career. We made plans to move in together in the Summer.

She wrote yet another letter: *"You deserve the best and I want to be the woman to give it to you and make you the happiest man on earth, nothing else and no one else will ever matter, just you and our love and this bond we share... I know we met for a reason and I know in my heart that you are the one for me."*

Deanna needed money for the rent and deposit on a new apartment, separate from Jay. She was still in debt from her jaunt at university. I went to the bank the next day and sent five hundred dollars via Western Union.

Deanna thanked me and insisted on paying me back.

It was a relief to do something concrete to prove I loved her. She said she felt safe knowing my love would always be there.

Deanna's fears started to dissipate. Then she split up with Jay. Well, for two weeks before she had sex with him again...

She called me, cried about it, and again said what a "coward" she was. He had left and was sleeping in his car outside.

I was angry but I said, in my monotone: "It's just a slip."

She was drunk: "WHYTHEFUCKARENTYERANGRY?"

I paused then said: "I don't know."

That made Deanna cough with laughter: "Ya dun know what we did to each other."

"As long as you didn't hit him, it'll be ok."

Then she was surly again: "YADONTUNDERSTAND."

"Deanna... Just sleep, ok?"

Now her voice was coy: "What if I don't want to?"

"Dee... did you hit him?"

"SHUT UP!" I had to hold the phone away from my ear. Deanna screamed: "SHUTUPYERFUCKENSLIMYMOUTH!"

Then the click of the phone as she hung up.

Later, she wrote a drunken email where she fully turned on me: *"Yr a fucken coward. Yr just like Jay."*

Something clicked. I downed some brandy and wrote she had behaved like: "A drunk cunt and a whore."

What was wrong with my binary brain? Thankfully she was too drunk to dial my lengthy number correctly. She lazily typed: *"i cant even fucken cal u yr crazy a loser and oversenstve. Never fycken swear at me agin."*

I emailed back, focusing my bleary eyes on the keyboard, then triple checking it before sending: "At least I have the fucking balls to do what I believe in." I paused for another moment then typed: "Good night."

The next day, I bunked my teaching job to call her. Deanna told me she had been waiting by the phone. I apologised, she apologised.

"Do ya still wanta marry me?" she said.

"Of course I do, you numpty."

"Numpty?"

"Ah..."

I started looking for a wedding ring the next day.

I had it made from my design – it had to be perfect. It was expensive and would take 6 weeks to make. It was in the shape of the infinity sign, with rubies on the crossband and diamonds underneath. Diamonds for eternity and rubies for fire.

The jeweller was exceptionally nice to me. He was mentally counting the hefty amount of money he'd soon receive.

Deanna said: "It sounds so, so beautiful," when I called her after I left the jeweller's.

I looked out of the window of the phone booth. A red eyed pigeon was flapping around and trying to fuck another pigeon. I described it to Deanna and said: "Can birds rape?"

She laughed as I let the receiver hang and I stomped off to break them up.

When I returned she was still laughing: "Are you done?"

"Yeah."

"I love you..."

33

Now that Jay was seemingly gone for good, I bought my ticket for my Summer break from teaching. As ever, my workload eased once it hit June and July. I longed to fill August with Deanna.

Deanna continued to say she felt terrified at the changes ahead, but also said she felt as happy as she ever had in her life.

I fell into marriage planning wholeheartedly – the correct flowers (yellow roses, white Japanese anemones), the correct dress (pearlised, lacy and over the shoulder), the correct church (cold and Catholic) and so on.

All of Deanna's letters gave me a sense of security. They were the unfiltered version of her, behind the annoying badass schick. She massaged my fragile ego: *"You're smart, charming, loving, compassionate, creative, and so damn beautiful, how could I not fall for you. Any other women would be a fool to pass you by. I want you to be mine, I want to show you what real love feels like. I want to be yr best friend, your heart, your soul, your wife."*

Yet, at the same time, Deanna started to go out more to dance and drink with her girlfriends. She would call me before she went out and I always made a point of wishing her a great time.

More letters and emails from Deanna followed that: *"Yr my beautiful angel who has brought a warm and kind light into my life and who continues to warm my spirit with each day I talk* to you. Just know that under all my fears and constant insecurities, I love you with everything I have. Yr future wife to be xoxoxo"

I drifted through my teaching job with a lunatic smile on my face. I had finally found happiness.

Deanna told me her workplace had sorted out the issue with violence. It made complete sense – "Health and Safety" had been a watchword at my college for years.

They had finally hired a stronger security guard to try to protect the staff from being attacked: "His mantra," Deanna laughed, "is CONTAIN AND CONTROL!!!" He sounded like a good guy, wrapping himself around the inmates/students when they exploded, and dragging them to the ground as quietly as possible.

She laughed and told me he seemed very white for a black man. Deanna said – almost idly – that the white/black guard was also teaching her how to use a manual gearbox. She was a psychotic driver and I told her that he was a miracle worker if he managed to teach her how to improve.

She was so happy and moving forward. Ah, if only I could have seen her smiling face other than through a computer screen.

I sent a dozen yellow roses for her birthday and called her.

"Thank you so much," she said, "they're beautiful."

"I'm glad."

"I've got a present for you too."

I could hear the buzz of a vibrator: "Just talk to me, ok?"

"Ok..."

So I did, my potty mouth being used to full effect.

As Deanna came she told me she loved me more than ever.

34

Then things started to change. I barely heard from her.

Had I been too filthy? Or had she grown bored of me?

The enigma of love is always unfathomable to decode.

I called Deanna from another booth, weeks later. She was in a hurry to go out and her mood was odd. She asked: "What if things don't work out... Wouldya still always be there for me?"

"Always," I exhaled slowly and probably for too long, "but why are you asking?"

"Quit it." Another change in tone, which was becoming her specialty: "You're trying to control me."

That was annoying: "I always want you to go out."

"Don't worry, ok?" I heard a door creak open. "I have to go now." Then she blew a kiss down the phone.

After I hung up the phone, I vomited. Then I had three almost sleepless nights fretting like an adolescent.

I wrote a drunken e-mail about how worried I was that she hadn't been in touch. How I hoped she wasn't ill, or that she had been arrested: "I know it's crazy but I worry..."

Deanna emailed later that night with one word: "Don't." In another email an hour later she told me to ring at a set time.

The first time, she wasn't there. I called 3 times, spaced over an hour. The last time I left a six word message: "It's Steve, ok? I love you."

She talked to me online that night.

She wrote: *"I haven't been going out with my girlfriends."*

"Oh, yeah?"

"I've met someone else." He had heard my phone message. He was the man who'd been teaching her how to stickshift.

It turned out she had been fucking him for a month.

I felt like my body had dropped. I couldn't breathe.

I said the three words I most regret in my life: "I need you."

Deanna wrote: *"It's wrong to be needy. You should want things instead."*

That niggled me: "Well, fuck, I want you then."

"I still love you, ok?" Then a harrumph. *"I don't want to, but I do."*

"So?"

"Can't we be best friends? Like soulmates?"

I had heard the line too many times before. I knew that all women sign a contract at aged 18. It states: *"If you are in a relationship, you cannot be friends with a straight, single man."*

It's not hard to figure out the reasons why, and again it made me wish – like my brother – I had been born gay. Being straight was a heavy weight on my balls.

I said: "That friendship is never going to happen, is it?"

"Fuck you."

"You wish."

35

Things became suitably nasty.

The next day I got an e-mail from Deanna's address.

It wasn't from her. Her new man had sent a moronic rant which finished by telling me: *"Do not to cross the line."*

I wrote back: "We're not in a Western." I didn't get a reply to that... so I christened him "The Meat" and wrote to Deanna telling her how betrayed I felt.

She replied: *"It's a free country!!! He can write what he likes!!!"*

The mutual whining continued. Deanna played my birthday gift down the phone.

It was a music box with the Charlie Brown theme, which she refused to send. To further confuse things, she did send me a cute birthday card. It had glitter and little bugs in the night sky. It said: *"You deserve nothing but goodness and happiness today and everyday for the rest of your life. Love, Deanna xxx"*

She told me it took an hour to pick out, but it didn't smell of her perfume.

Academic

Partly as revenge, I picked up her wedding ring from the jeweller's. He had an open smile as I handed over the cheque for rocks and gold. I wrote Deanna a letter about how it felt for me to get it. I was working on a passive-aggressive streak of my own...

She wrote back: *"I already talked to him... and he said as long as you didn't bother me, then he would leave you alone. The ring sounds really beautiful, I cried when I read about it, I'm sorry I'm such an ass, I wish I could see it. I can't believe I did this to you... I want you to know that you are always in my heart, ALWAYS. Thank you for everything you have done for me... I know one day you will find the woman you are meant to be with... You deserve the best, I'm sorry I let you down in so many ways."*

I simply told her: "Look, Deanna, I won't visit unless you want me to."

She wrote another bi-polar e-mail in response: *"If I said fuck off you still wouldn't. JUST TELL ME THE TRUTH!!! I know you...!!! and I know you would go out of yr way to find me and see me why are you denying that!!!! No more "I'll fuck off if you want me to" because I know you never will. You promised me you wouldn't ever and I know you would do anything for me... admit I'm right! that you would go to no ends for me, that you would hunt me down and tell me how much you need and love me!!! it's true and you know it and I can feel it burning inside myself!!!"*

The emails and phone calls continued, of course. Whenever Deanna would get drunk she would send lengthy messages: *"Come see me. You will leave NY knowing you have a best friend, a woman, a soulmate who cares for you deeply... You mean a lot to me, more than I want to admit, I will tell you that your love does and did scare me. I wish I wasn't so afraid all the time. I only want happiness for you always. You are beautiful and so is yr writing and I miss sharing our words together."*

I'll admit I liked the revenge of not sending her any stories and I also I suspected she was showing everything to her boyfriend. I politely asked her during a phone conversation: "Have you shown all of my emails and letters to The Meat?"

"DON'T CALL HIM THAT!" She screamed: "AND NO!!!"

"Is he in the room right now?"

I knew the truth as her voice trailed off: "No..."

36

Further phone conversations and emails from Deanna kept asking me if I would still bring the engagement ring with me. I said yes, and I admitted I loved her as much as ever.

In response, Deanna sent me a poem about The Meat:

I haven't been able to cum
In three days -
Yet his body
Is the most beautiful
Thing to me -
My African King who

Academic

Yields at nothing to fill
Me with pleasure
Up against the wall
My dress pinned behind
My ears after a long day in the sun
My body saturated with sweat
Dripping out of my pours,
His tongue working the salt
Off my skin from our ocean
Kiss
My mind can't focus
This dam light catches into my eyes
And my brain can't slow down enough
To enjoy his mouth on my pussy
I moan and gasp inbetween for breaths
His ego in one hand
And his cock in the other
My nails begin to dig into his
Spine as I watch his ass shift
Up and down I see the fine ass
Of all his ancestors in Ghana
And begin to wonder if any of
The women there had problems
Like this -
He thrusts his hips into mine
I can feel the warmth of the

Summer heat envelop us
I take a small bite
Out of his shoulder
"I'm almost there" I thought
Not wanting to admit I was Never
Even half way there……

I didn't tell her that her writing had become even more ghastly. And who the fuck was I to complain? I wasn't doing anything except teaching and drinking heavily. As I lost myself in thought, not one word would come to my computer screen.

Then Deanna drunkenly emailed the eternal lines: *"Just sucked off my African King n his bud from copschool. Can still taste there black cum in my mouth."*

Did that make her racist or progressive? It certainly made her a reverse-sexist cunt.

"I'm so sorry," she wrote in the morning. *"I MISS YOU!!!"*

Ah, fuck it. I bought two plane tickets for myself and my friend, Thomas Salter.

Might as well flame out in a blaze of abject horror...

37

Deanna called me every night in the hotel room. The little red light was permanently flashing over the first week I returned from exploring New York.

"I hope you've had a good day," she said. "I... I'll call later. 'bout 9.30, ok, honey?"

At spot-on 9.30pm, I was tired from jetlag, tired from walking and tired of thinking about her. I mumbled through an hour long conversation but just the sound of her voice was the like the sweet Irish whiskey I supped throughout.

Her voice slurred towards the end of the conversation too: "Do you love me, Steve?"

"Deanna..."

"DO YOU?"

I rested my head against the receiver and laid down: "I don't want to talk about it." This was becoming a Kafkaesque conversation where I knew no answer would be the right one.

Deanna said softly: "I'm sorry, ok..." then she would start to whisper: "I want you to tell me. So I know."

She knew the answer, but the same dance had to happen. Was it my punishment for loving her, or my way of punishing her?

She got mock angry, emphasising her New York accent in a coo-coo voice: "I'm not comin' to seeya. I don't wanna seeya."

"That's fine."

Then her trademark shift in tone: "I KNOW you CAN'T not see me." I could almost hear her chin jutting out in defiance. "You'll hunt me down."

"No, I won't. I said I wouldn't."

"You WILL."

"We'll see."

"I'm gonna hang up."

"Deanna," I said with resignation, "you won't."

Thomas was snoring in our hotel room... but was he really asleep? The noisiest air conditioner in New York gurgled away but failed to drown out his drone.

Deanna asked: "Ya want me to hang up?"

"No," I shut my eyes and hoped something would change when I opened them: "I don't."

"Awwww..."

This was madness and it only got worse. Four hot nights later, Thomas went to the toilet to vomit some leftover KFC.

The light on the phone lit up again.

Deanna said: "Hello, beautiful."

I said: "Hmm."

Now I could speak freely I told Deanna that I loved her. Even as the words came out, I regretted telling the truth.

She cooed with delight: "Awww... Baby... I..."

In all those phone calls, over all the time, it still drove me wild. No-one had ever said they loved me and truly meant it.

I asked her to repeat it, and she paused for effect, then: "Steve, I love you."

That was her power: "Hmm."

"When do you want to meet me?"

"Soon," I said, cradling the phone against my ear, "it seems dumb to meet you three weeks in."

Academic

"You'll come and see me before then... I KNOW you will... You'll come and see me..."

"I won't do anything you don't want me to. I promised."

"You want to come!"

"I do." I rubbed my forehead. "But only when you say."

I still had hope boiling away. There were three weeks before the flight home... enough time to sort everything out.

"See me on Sunday, ok?"

"Alright, Deanna."

"It'll give me time to recover from work..."

By then I was almost fully asleep but with the phone still in my hand: "I love you."

38

Thomas and I woke up early on that Sunday. I was shivering straight away, even though I wasn't cold. Was it dehydration?

It was still too hot. The sun gouged my eyes out when I pulled up the blind. Our room backed on to an ugly, semi-stuccoed building opposite. The fucking thing seemed to amplify light.

We took Absente shots. It was a cheap, watered down version of Absinthe. Still 60%, but with safer wormwood. I rested it underneath my tongue and enjoyed it lighting up my mouth.

I didn't feel drunk, but my mouth felt very dry.

It was still early. Maybe 11? The train was at 12.57.

I mixed 50% Black Smirnoff and coke in a bottle and the wave of heat struck hit me as I left the foyer.

We got the bus down. I put the Metrocard in the wrong way but the driver wasn't an asshole about it. Then it was Grand Central, which was always a treat. A baffling dome of beauty and detail. I craned my neck back at the sky-high, beautiful, Beaux-Arts' ceilings. A place to scream without being heard...

Deanna had sent train times for the Long Island Express. We got down into the subway and the analogue time-boards looked like something from the thirties. Crowds stared at the boards as they clicked over... then they rushed off in panic.

About 20 minutes in, "Long Island" turned around. The mass of ants rushed to the left through double doors.

We walked after slowly and Thomas said: "I think the planners probably factored in people who walk slowly..."

The train was still there. It made me think of Japan. Sleek, silver, with a high place to sit. We nestled into those seats and shared shots of the vodka and coke. A conductor took our tickets. He was friendly and completely unconcerned about the booze.

Thomas asked me: "You nervous?"

I took a long gulp from the bottle and said: "Hmm."

I went to the toilet 5 times during the journey. It was beautiful in there... very clean with the sheen of stainless steel.

The last time I defecated I looked into the steel door as the remnants of my guts and bladder dribbled out. My reflection made me laugh. It was the face of insanity. I was there but floating above. I watched and heard all of it, every detail, every sound.

I counted down the stops on the digital board above the stairs. At each stop I wished it wouldn't reach the next one.

Thomas said: "I thought you said Long Island was close to New York."

"20, 30 miles?"

"This is more like 80."

We traded shots from the bottle as people got on and off the train. Eventually we pulled into the final stop. We had finished the bottle 20 minutes before and now I was worried I'd sober up.

The car park was completely empty.

I looked around.

"You see anything?" Thomas asked.

"They'll be here."

We wandered around an empty building. It looked like it had been closed for years. Maybe we had come to the wrong place? I didn't want to be the one who had messed up...

Thomas said: "Hey," and nudged me.

A small car pulled up. The driver was obviously Misha, and Deanna peered out shyly from the passenger seat.

I must have looked strangely back because she quickly said something to her best gal-pal.

We walked over and both of them got out of the car.

"Well, hey there you." Deanna smiled as she said it.

She was so much shorter than I remembered. She was wearing trainers and pedal-pushers. She had said on the phone she might wear them because she had "been feeling fat."

The black diaphanous top still looked great. It was high necked and cut across her chest like a cross-your-heart bra. Her tits looked big and I didn't give a fuck about a little fat around her gut. I should have said it, or maybe I shouldn't?

I opted to tilt my head and smile. I said: "Hello you." Her doe-eyes had a unique mix of blue and green. Deanna quickly looked down, but I could see her smiling as she did.

I held out my hands and she grabbed around my waist quickly. She didn't hold on for long, and I didn't hold her. Maybe I should have done that too?

Deanna pulled the car-chair forward so we could get in. We said "Hi" to Misha and she was so much blander than the photos Deanna had sent. A stultified face caked in foundation.

Deanna faced forward as Thomas and I made small talk with Misha as she scooted along the roads with an easy knowledge but a bored voice.

I looked at Deanna the whole way. I could see her looking in the wing mirror and glance down into it and smile.

Her hair looked good. Very thick and not too bright like before. It was down and mid-brown with a hint of red. She'd clearly washed it beforehand. I wanted to stroke it, but I wanted to talk the night away, like we had a hundred times before.

I smiled a goofy, stupid smile.

39

We arrived at another car park. Deanna kept out in front and talked to Misha, who ordered us to follow them. We walked to some place next to the water, but it was closed.

Eventually we got to some club. It was a sad American-Mexican pastiche of numberplates, hubcaps and prints of cacti.

Misha crammed her way to the packed bar and ordered the booze... Coronas with limes shoved in the necks. I didn't know what to do with it so pushed it in. Deanna left the lime up top.

Misha won on some scratchcard and the drinks were half price. I offered her money but she refused it dismissively: "Let's find somewhere to sit." There was something elusive about Misha's voice and personality that felt something like danger.

Deanna sat opposite Thomas and not me. I had sat first, so I guessed she wanted it that way. But I... I...

More conversation and a childlike menu of shit food. A couple of times Deanna mouthed "What?" and then smiled down at the table.

She was thinking that I found her as beautiful as ever, and was shy about it. Her skin was pock-marked, her teeth were fucked up. I loved her completely so why wouldn't she let me say it?

I was wearing the Dolphins shirt, like the first time, and she was in her same top too. I felt confident she found me attractive. Even with Lanny or Tara, I had never fully believed it before.

They served crab legs and croquettes filled with cheese.

Thomas said: "Everything here has fucking cheese in it!"

Deanna said: "Cheese is good for you."

"High in calcium," Misha joined in.

Deanna didn't eat any of the food. Her stomach was probably heaving, as she said it would. The crab legs were awkward to eat. I had some of the cheese thing, but the sauce was so strong it was like swallowing bile.

Misha and Thomas crunched, chewed, and sucked away.

"So, you like Bukowski then?" Thomas asked.

"Yeah," Deanna replied.

Deanna sat back, cowering behind Misha.

"And you've read Kerouac too?"

"Yeah," she said. "Ah went to his grave one time."

I tried to extract something more: "Did you like those Fante books I sent?"

"Yeah," then Deanna stared at me with a deliberate coyness and then smiled, "Ah did. Really."

She had some hushed conversation with Misha and seemed to loosen up. There was twenty minutes of empty talk until Deanna said: "Ah need a cigarette."

I said: "Ok."

"You wanna come out with me?"

"Yeah."

I followed her outside and she lit a filtered Camel. She looked at me and pouted her lips. With the wind cutting in from the sand, Deanna took long drags from her cigarette then said: "Don't look at me like that..."

I looked back blankly.

She said: "What?" with a mock baby voice.

"You keep doing that. Looking at me..."

"I can't help it that I find you beautiful."

I felt so happy that I even smiled: "Ditto."

"Thank you." She looked down, tapped her cigarette, then when she looked up she had a beaming smile.

I was tired of dodging feelings. I pulled her in and hugged her. She gripped tightly and she said: "You're so beautiful."

I said: "Ha." Deanna was always a lousy judge of looks: "Is it the Miami shirt?"

"Iz everythin'... you dis'pointed in me?"

She was bigger and I was skinnier. We broke out even. "No."

"Have ah changed?"

"No."

She was wide-eyed and smiling: "Thank you."

I said the usual cliché: "Your eyes are so very beautiful."

Her closed smile again... no teeth showing, like the hundreds of photos she had sent me: "You like my outfit?"

The outfit was far from accidental: "Your tits always look damn good in that top..."

"HEY!" Again, baby voice. Gravelly this time: "What about these tit-tays..." Deanna grabbed my left nipple and twisted it.

"Ow!"

"Pfffft," she said and lit another cigarette. Another woman came out. She must have heard my accent because she asked me if I'd been surprised at the rudeness of New York. I said how everyone has been very polite and I wished she would go away...

There was a planter full of sand where everyone stubbed out their cigarettes. Deanna was wearing some pale blue eye shadow, a little lipstick, some foundation. Little lumps of acne showed in the light. I wanted to stroke her face to show everything was more than ok.

As the woman left, Deanna tweaked my nipple again, and laughed: "Whut rrrrrrrrrrr ya lookin' at?"

"You."

I pulled her in for another hug. I felt the need to draw her inside me. She said: "Hey! Ah'm tryin' to smoke here!" Her cigarette fell to one side and she gripped me with the other arm.

Deanna smiled: "Lez go back inside," then she tweaked my nipple again and she held my hand as we walked inside.

40

Thomas and Misha turned to face us. What had they been talking about? What were they thinking? Why did I care?

Deanna tweaked my nipple again and giggled, then she followed Misha to buy more booze. Again, there were more unheard words.

I stood feeling awkward and Thomas finished off his Corona with a look swig. He said: "There's something going on..."

I said: "Ah, it's ok."

Misha came back, and handed out the drinks.

I asked: "Win anything this time?"

"Half price again. My lucky day." Her face was devoid of any emotion. I sensed mild disdain but nothing else.

It was getting darker outside. It had felt like 30 minutes but it had been 2 hours. Now I hoped everything didn't end soon.

"We're going to..." Misha said. Some bar. Urgh, why not?

We followed dutifully and the cold twilight struck me as strange. Deanna tweaked my nipple again as we walked down another road: "You cold, huh?"

I tweaked her nipple back and she said: "Hey!"

She looked down at her tits and held her hands underneath them and raised them up. She smiled and tweaked my left nipple once again. We walked off, this time Deanna was with me, while Thomas was with Misha and some other girl.

Deanna said: "That's Dino."

"Ok."

She held my hand: "The one that talks all the time…"

"Yeah?" Strange thoughts rattled in my empty head.

We walked until we were back at Misha's car. Some other car was sitting nearby and Dino went into that one.

As we travelled along, Misha complained about her car, and Deanna asked if there was enough room. Thomas and I smiled and said, knees close to our chins but almost in unison: "It's fine."

I felt the first surge of depression wave over me in the next bar. It was something depressing about the jukebox and the lonely man stood behind the bar. He was a barman lost in space.

There were two women at the bar that greeted Deanna.

There was a toilet and I went into it. I felt drunk, but I wasn't happy. I sat there for some time…

They were all waiting when I emerged. There was another bottle of Corona sitting there. I had the vague feeling I'd paid for it but I didn't remember handing over the money.

We walked outside and the air was damp and hot. There were some people already there and Deanna waved to greet them. Everyone's voices became moronic and indecipherable.

Deanna talked to the group. She had told them that I was the "English Guy." Some looked at me. Dino smiled, but the rest of the facial expressions were impossible to work out. Then there were loud laughs and hushed conversations that I couldn't hear.

Thomas and I shared meaningless smalltalk before, mercifully, Dino came over. She sat down and smiled. She had broadly spaced eyes and dark brown hair with a blunt fringe. She said: "They're so noisy!" She was very cute.

"They certainly are," said Thomas.

"Are you ok?" she asked me.

"Always," I replied and I felt very drunk.

Dino never rambled and talked intelligently. It was talk about our adventures in New York, and we got on well.

Thomas took a photo of Dino, then a shot of Misha. Dino hugged me, then Deanna got up and had her photo taken with me. I couldn't smile and I said the photo would be fucking terrible...

I felt incredibly tired and my head had become heavy.

I went to the bar to buy another drink.

I came back and Deanna was there.

41

I said nothing again. I felt a surge of love and hugged her.

Deanna said my name and whined: "No..." She looked outside, where her friends were.

I said: "I don't care what they think."

"...I have someone already. You know that."

She seemed so tiny. I wished she had worn heels.

I walked back with her, dropped off the drink with Thomas. He pursed his lips and sensed something was happening.

I walked back to the toilet. The light was off and somehow that soothed me. I think it was the woman's toilet, but I couldn't see anything else.

The light started to flick on and off. I ignored it. It did it again... She cooed my name then: "He-ey..."

"Hey, Deanna."

She flicked the light on and off again.

"If I wanted to start a seizure..."

"You like that...?" Her gravelly voice made me smile.

I came outside and she was in the doorway. She posed coquettishly and growled something like: "Cummmmmoutside..."

"What was that?"

"Jus' cum outside."

We stood in the same corridor as before.

I said: "I love you."

Deanna looked up at me again and whispered "Steve..." She clasped her fingers into mine, then levered out as she said: "Let's dance."

I drew her back in, lightly, and said: "I don't like dancing."

She let go of one hand, and spun out on the other in the style of a Viennese waltz. Then she wrapped herself around me.

I remember... oh, why the fuck do I remember everything?

Misha came through the door and said: "What're ya doin'?"

Academic

Deanna withdrew from me. "Come on..." Deanna led me outside, releasing her hand as soon as she left the doorway.

Again we sat at different tables, with more jabber. Then as soon as Thomas walked to the toilet, Deanna took his seat.

She said: "We need to talk..."

I cried. She hadn't even said it yet but I was crying already.

The garishness hit me. Some fattie, Misha, Dino and the others were on the other table and yet they paid no attention to Deanna's absence. Had she already told them what she was going to do? They continued their incoherent talk, as if we weren't there.

Deanna turned and joined in their conversation as my eyes watered. My face felt normal, but I could feel the tears pour out and they were stinging my eyes.

She turned back to me again, and Thomas returned. He sat down to my left, looking but not looking...

Deanna stared at me: "I needta tell ya that I'm with my guy now."

"But..."

"I wan' us to be friends, but I have my guy now."

"But I love you."

She looked at me throughout, yet there was no recognition I was crying. A touch of the hand? Something?

"I need you," I choked. I expected anger back.

"You don't NEED anyone... I told you that," she said.

I wiped my face and noted how wet it felt. Something woke up inside me. I smiled and said: "Urgh... I'm sorry."

"I want us to be friends, ok?"

"You promise not to leave me?" What a fucktard I was...

"JEEZ! Where will I go?" She looked to the skies: "Ok?"

Still, we didn't touch and the people continued to talk.

Still, Thomas was watching but not watching.

The air was now free of cloud and midnight blue. I felt empty, and there were no more tears left.

42

Deanna resumed full-blown conversation with the other people and Thomas and I talked as if nothing had happened.

Eventually Misha came over with her scowl: "Gotta get back to the station..."

We left, and Deanna said "bye" to the other people, including Dino. Dino smiled and said "bye" to us. She was a beautiful spark of true life and solidity.

I said: "Bye" and felt ashamed, but there was nothing that even suggested they'd noticed me crying.

We got in the cramped car again. I felt odd, but fine.

I said with wide-eyed innocence: "Maybe we can go to the baseball cage next time?"

"Sure, maybe next time," Misha said.

Deanna said: "I'll have to hit every one before we go!"

"It'd be fun, huh?" I said and turned to Thomas.

He tilted his head slightly: "Maybe."

We reached the station. Misha got out and flipped her seat forward. Thomas and I squeezed out.

Deanna was waiting next to the door. I felt shy again and raised one hand up in a little wave: "Well, er, bye."

She looked up at me and whispered: "Oh, Steve..."

"Um, call?" I murmured.

She stood closer to me: "Don't be like that."

I gently hugged her and I loved her again. Deanna gripped on to me tightly. As she walked off my brain noted her clothes were strange. She looked 30, and yet they looked 20. I then looked down at myself and the wreck I had become.

I didn't see her get back in the car, but I held up my hand as she left. Deanna waved once and Misha smiled an empty smile. I thought about how little impact Misha had made on me. I knew she was dating an ex-drug dealer, so I had hoped for some fire.

I could see Deanna talk to her as the car pulled to the left, drove out and away. I didn't follow it, because I looked up at the sky instead. It was still that odd blue colour, so light yet so dark.

Thomas said: "Wake up, Steve."

I looked around and the station was completely empty and suspiciously clean.

Some sort of void seemed to close around me.

Hmm.

43

The air was warm and it didn't feel like night at all. There was no wind. I said: "Where's the train?"

"I don't know," Thomas said, "we're on time..."

Deanna had told me the train was due in 5 minutes.

Thomas asked: "Are you ok?"

"Sure."

I walked over to the platform and sat down.

It was a very flat and the blue marble was refreshingly cool.

Ten minutes passed.

Nothing.

I asked: "Do you think we missed it?"

"Nah."

Ten more minutes passed. A guy with one leg rounded the corner and swung towards us on crutches. He stopped and stayed in front of the station-house. Then he turned to look at us but he said nothing. I mentally urged him to pull a gun.

Thomas went over to him. He offered him a cigarette, which the man took. He looked stunned when Thomas asked him where the train was.

The crippled man said: "Iz loooong goowne, ma friend..."

I laid face down and fully stretched out. The cold spread through me and a pressing weight pinned my body into the marble.

Thomas returned, sat on a bench and started smoking a cigarette. The crippled man swung away to his own life. Thomas said: "It's times like this you remember."

The train didn't come but the deathly weight on my shoulders did. I laid face down on the marble platform and cried, not knowing why. I watched the domes of water where the tears had settled.

Thomas was right. You remove hope and you build sense. Nothing is more liberating than having no hope. All of the inane seriousness of life melts away, and you ride it for all it's worth.

Thomas got up and prodded my shoulder: "Wake up!"

"Slap me," I said.

"What?"

"Slap me."

He stubbed out his cigarette into the marble and slapped me across the face. It hurt much more than I thought it would.

Thomas looked at me: "You never remember the good stuff, just the shit. The *truly* shit. That's when you feel most alive."

"Let's get home." My mind was active again: "Call Misha."

I only heard Thomas's end of the conversation: "Yeah... the train's failed to arrive... could ya come and give us a lift... yeah, yeah... no, not really... Err, ok. Yeah, bye."

"So?" I asked.

"She's not coming. She says to get a bus."

"There aren't any buses in the middle of the fucking night."

"I know," Thomas said, "she really didn't want to come."

"She was a little strange..."

"More than that," he said, "so let's get a taxi."

We wandered into the centre of whatever part of Long Island we were stranded in. I heard what I thought were gunshots and voices riding on the breeze, but the streets were empty.

I looked in my wallet and realised I had hardly any money. We walked some more, and there was a bank. I took out 80 bucks and Thomas called a number he found in a phone booth.

The taxi came and the driver was shocked to see two dimwitted Brits. We told him to drive us to the next station. We guessed it was 20, 30, 40 miles away? Oh, fuck all this, just let me sleep.

The arched eyebrow seemed to suspect we were gay: "That'll be 50 bucks, guys, ok?"

"Sure."

My eyes burned as I looked out the window for the entire journey. None of us talked. We passed a service station. A man was strutting around in front of his friends as if he was holding a weapon. But no-one ran out and there was no screaming.

Then there were wide roads and buildings. Time flowed and I was no longer aware of it.

We got to the next station, and somehow the train was there. It was an older train, like the ones on the subway. The train must have only left from this station on its final run into New York.

The ride through the bleached landscape took a lot less time than the trip out. I hoped there was a message from Deanna on the phone when I got back.

I laid down on the seat and ended up crying some more. Thomas took photos of me and time passed so fucking quickly...

44

We walked back to our hotel from Grand Central Station. I kept walking simply because Thomas was walking.

A rare yellow cab swooshed by on the road. The air was still and calm. The city that never sleeps was asleep. But I was still awake. I was... I am still... I think... Or am I?

A block from the hotel a bum walked towards us. He was going to pull a knife. He was the ideal candidate. He was dirty, bearded and in rags. I wanted him to mug us...

The bum stopped directly in front of us. He asked, very politely: "Can you spare some change please?"

Thomas said: "Sure" and pulled out two crumpled dollar bills from his pocket.

The bum said: "Thank you kindly," and shambled onwards.

Oh, fuck it.

The foyer to our hotel was empty. The lift was empty. The corridor was empty. It was sometime after 4am.

Thomas opened our hotel door, and I looked down at the phone. The little red light was flickering.

Deanna must have called to ask me if we had got back ok. I peeled off my shoes and socks, and called the voicemail number.

There was a man's voice: "Hello... Remember me?"

My heart sighed but the rest of me listened.

"You did a real bad thing tonight... The line has been crossed. I'm coming for you now."

I suddenly wanted to laugh: "Come and hear this, Thomas," and I called the number again.

I believed it would be different that time. It was only when we listened to it again that it felt like a punch to my gut.

"Troublesome," Thomas said, "and utter bullshit."

He laid on his mattress and I laid face down on the bed.

Sleep and strange dreams came surprisingly easily.

45

The next day I was on the roof of the hotel. I checked my e-mail. There was a message from Deanna and another from The Meat, sent shortly after each other.

Deanna said she had been at work and thought about how disappointed she was in me. She had been wondering if women in Britain like to be manhandled, and was appalled I *"grabbed her breast"* and kept hugging her. She said I was arrogant and talked all the time. Deanna then said I was manipulative for crying, and that I was an attention seeker. She said she wondered if she wanted to be friends with me anymore.

The Meat said that I *"better keep away and go back to England if I knew what was good for me."* He accused me of assault. He wrote that he heard Thomas was a really nice guy and hoped that I hadn't ruined his holiday. He then said he would *"feed the hobnobs to his dog"* and called the Royal Family *"gay."*

Ah...

Well, the Royal Family bored me and there was nothing about Britishness that appealed to me. Precious little appealed to me about life in general...

I wrote an e-mail back to each of these monstrosities.

To him: I lightly mocked what he had said about me and told him not to worry anymore. I would go, as I promised her. Not because of the threats, but because she had essentially told me to.

To Deanna: My hands lingered over the keyboard. I STILL loved her... and not as a masochist. I loved the memory of that pure love, and I didn't want to be a victim. So, to her, I was NICE...

I said I was confused that she took the nipple twist as some kind of molestation, considering how many times she had twisted mine. I wrote that I thought she wanted me to hug her, by the way she kept looking at me and gripped around me. I told her I didn't know how to act, and that I was sorry I offended her.

More mechanical words from a mechanical brain.

I wrote that I would keep my promise, as all the promises I kept before, and not speak to Deanna again. I typed: "Goodbye."

I walked outside and Thomas was sitting on the rooftop terrace. I sat next to him and it was stiflingly humid. The Empire State Building was glinting in the sun.

I said: "The Empire State Building looks good."

Thomas said: "That's not the Empire State Building."

I hated the sun and now I hated the Rockefeller Building.

I wanted to suck it all inside me until I was surrounded by darkness and the purity of the night.

46

After I returned to college following New York, I was down to a couple of hours sleep a night. Even with booze to help, the pounding thoughts about Deanna continued to destroy my sanity.

I left an old e-mail address open and checked it every day. She e-mailed five months later. My heart pounded and I breathed in hard before I opened it.

She had written one word: *"Sorry."*

How I wanted to fucking respond to that...

After that, I got the shakes and I couldn't find any peace in my head. I knew I had to keep Deanna away, but my old insanity was back and the next year of teaching was intensely obsessive.

Academic

I demanded perfection and I'd scrawl over essays and pick up every typo or lack of evidence. I could spend an hour on each essay.

I tried to be pleasant, but the wick had been lit. Sparks started spraying from my mouth with attacks on the college's lies about "professionalism" and "distance."

I knew there were teachers fucking students. I knew there were awful teachers, and I knew there were awful students. In both cases, they seemed to get away with it because money was involved. I knew every student represented £2000 to the Catholic and cuntish Head of Finance who had never taught a lesson in his life.

I taught an entire lesson – complete with examples from druggie films – on why one student (a half-arsed drug-dealing loudmouthed cock of a boy) was a dickhead instead of the hero students had made him into.

These low-level rants continued. Perfectly logical and justified... and they bought respect too. I already knew that one rant a year meant no student dared to fuck with you.

The rants were mostly directed at guys. A spotty fuck turning up drunk and playing with a beach-ball. Another pube-haired moron who kept making wacky animal noises. A raft of potheads with zero concentration and boring yap over Pink Floyd.

But they were small scale... 3.2 on the Ritcher Scale.

I was honing a burst of pent-up shit spat out in a few minutes of truth.

Academic

She was called Vikki Adams. She'd sit in lessons and face the other way. She was blonde with tiny evil eyes, a pig face and Saturday night make-up. I'd hear tales from the students and I knew she was a three-hole cumsack for various guys. But that didn't matter at all. I marked her half-arsed essays diligently, I tried to offer help, but she wasn't trying at all. She was vile, aloof, arrogant, rude and stupid... a whore trying to act the lady and failing at both.

The killer was that I caught her mocking the pregnant young woman in her class. Three times over three different lessons I saw Vikki puff out her cheeks and put her hands around her belly. The pothead who sat next to her laughed and enabled that vile human being.

A savvy student named Ally had told me Vikki been badmouthing me to other students: "She's a giant cunnie, ok?" Then she blew a raspberry through her fingers and giggled.

"Yeah, Al," I smiled. "I know."

So in the next infamous lesson, Vikki ambled in, sat down and faced the other way. She started talking to the pothead again and puffing out her cheeks and rubbing her stomach...

I could see the pregnant student was on the verge of tears.

"TURN THE HELL AROUND, VIKKI!"

She looked and me and whispered: "Fuck you."

"NO FUCK YOU, YOU CUNT... FUCK YOU! YOU FUCKING RUDE PIECE OF SHIT!"

The other students became completely silent... I closed in and she looked at me with total indifference.

"FUCK YOU, YOU PIECE OF SHIT! YOU DISGUST ME."

She flipped her hand at me to say "Whatever..."

"DON'T YOU FUCKING DO THAT... YOU DISGUSTING WASTE OF SKIN... GET THE FUCK OUT OF MY ROOM!"

Now she was a little stunned.

I bent over and screamed in her face: "NOW!"

She rushed out.

I watched the door ease shut, walked over to my desk and sat down. I looked at the group. Most of their mouths were gaping open. Then half of them – including the pregnant gal – broke into a round of applause.

What was I becoming? It would be foolish to blame all of it on Deanna. I still had my own mind somewhere in there. All I knew was I hated it, and that I needed to do *something*...

47

Each paycheck brought me nearer to saying: "I quit."

Fantasies raged. I would storm in and slap down the letter on Wilson's desk and *laugh*... no, no, I'd scream "I QUIT!" in front of everyone... no, no, I'd film it, hide a camera and tell him exactly what a half-arsed cunt he was... no, no, a testament to make him sit up and notice. Enough to make him *sob* at the truth.

Finally I had enough to live, to travel, to pay for my rent and my food and booze. I wanted to take another stab at writing, but I also wanted to sort out all the shit at home and my relationship with a woman named Tara.

I rapped on Wilson's door and ambled in: "I'm leaving at the end of the academic year." As ever, his chair was overly high.

"Really?" He looked almost shocked. "Take a seat."

I sat, as upright as possible on my pee-wee chair: "I have other things I want to do."

"Well, we'll certainly miss your students' grades."

"Hmm."

"Can I do anything for you? Will you need a reference?"

Everything crashed in my head. Where was the confrontation... why is he... maybe I do need a reference... I'll need a job sometime... why is he not... job, job, damnit, money, fuckit...

"Well, yeah," I smiled weakly, "I guess."

Wilson told me about the future of the college, the building work, the investments... I didn't listen. I knew the moment had gone and I just wanted to get the hell out of there.

He'd won and I didn't say a word. Not then, not when I left.

And, of course, I had to look at Deanna's profile on AOL that night. Under occupation it said: "Writer/Dreamer/Social Worker & a soon to be mommy in October!!!"

I started to drink and remembered everything again...

Academic

After I wrote it all down – every memory that bubbled up in my dreams – I finally started to get my shit together.

It took two years.

But once it was all on the page, I could face teaching all over again.

48

Ultimately, the move was 100% correct. I missed yakking about films, and I was also near the poverty line. Teaching meant I could work the least hours for the most money.

I was screwed out of thousands by Thomas Salter through buying CDs and records for the Murder Slim Store. I'd foolishly believed in a increasingly overweight egotist who said: "Nothing is going to be better than this! We can sell books AND music!"

I felt even more sorry for his drug-addled father who spent months converting the store from a dilapidated hovel into something that could pass building regulations.

Thomas delayed opening the shop for month after month. It transpired he had been selling stock to friends and spending money on himself.

He wanted pear wine to drink and an oily rag to sniff. Above all, Thomas wanted to look like a hero to his cronies. The guy had always loved to rant about his own magnificence and now he could do so while doling out great, cut-price music.

Academic

I re-applied for the BTEC Media job when my college advertised it in January. No reply. Three months later another advert appeared with: "Previous applicants need not reapply... your application will automatically be considered." Nothing again.

During the summer break, the position came up again. I knew BTEC Media was much more "practical." You helped students make films rather than simply analyse them. This let students understand the hard process of film-making and gain a true appreciation of the form. It also meant I could teach how to create low-budget gore effects... and what's more fun than fake-vomiting in front of a class full of kids? After Doctor Devgan, Thomas and Deanna, I'd had plenty of practice at getting my puke mix just right.

I had little to lose, so I wrote an aggressive letter demanding to know what was going on. I argued that they knew I could turn up the next day and teach effective lessons...

"Ok, old chap, come in tomorrow," Wilson wrote. "Don't stay up too late!!!"

Ah... now I suspected the alcoholic shtick was behind it.

I did – and still do – drink. Much more than is medically ok. But I have *never* drunk to the point of stupor... no-one has ever seen me shit-faced. I also never drank before – or during – teaching during my first stint at college.

Unfortunately, I had fucked up a key aspect when it comes to dealing with other teachers. *Never trust them.* Never show any side of your personality that could be used as a weapon. This would be used to impress their friends and their superiors. The huge amount of management posts meant that it was an ugly case of survival of the most sarcastic and the most career driven.

I'd been naïve enough to attend a party a few weeks before I was due to quit. I had already handed in my notice, and my summer birthday meant that it hit on a day when I had the afternoon off. I trotted down the pub with some friends and the friendliest of my students.

We had a high ol' time, full of the usual round of entertainingly sick stories. Everyone was over-18, so we weren't getting into illegal territory. Yeah, one of my friends projectile vomited... but where was the fun in drinking without a little projectile vomit?

Everything was going fine until the college's Dance teacher walked past. Harriet was a new teacher and eager to climb the ladder. She was revered as pretty, but I never understood why. She looked bland if kindly, with a long face and dead eyes that showed much more than the easy smile she liked to flash.

She – badly – acted surprised at us sitting in the bench outside the pub. But I fell for it and waved her over. Looking back, she'd obviously got some tip-off that I was there.

"Having a good time?"

"Yep!" People chimed in.

I said: "Have a drink with us." I was a fucking idiot.

Harriet didn't drink any booze but watched with interest for an hour. She happily joined in with various conversations.

Harried seemed so unconcerned and content, I thought I'd misjudged her. My students and my friends warmed to her. She went back to work, and we all went home after a few hours. No harm done, aside from me catching sunburn.

Shit, why was I even quitting teaching? It had been a good day.

Well, the next day wasn't. From the moment I walked into the morning meeting, suddenly younger teachers were looking at me. Oddly too and smirking sometimes. Harriet gave me a particularly smug look, and whispered to the Music Technology teacher next to her. They both gave a little laugh. Hmm...

A good number of the older teachers looked at me as if I'd just dumped in their mouths. I often wondered why the gossip-mill churns so quickly. The standard answer is they find their lives so boring that they seek out shit to smear over it and spice it up. It was a repellent, middle-class form of caprophagia.

By bitching about other people, they justify themselves. They want promotion. They want to bury any outside thoughts. The best way to define *professionalism* is to decry anything outside of the suit, the tie, and the distance from the students.

Within a week, the shitmill had probably ground me into not only being a drunk but also one caught in some mythical gangbang outside of the pub. In their fantasies, I was eating out a 16 year old while a male student licked my ass and another gal fellated me. They'd express it in prettier ways than that, but

Academic

gossip is gossip… tiresome, false and tedious. But as I repeatedly reapplied for my job I knew that some of the shit must have stuck.

The booze issue reminded me of what I feared when I started teaching. I was young, male, white, and apolitical. I was an easy target, and before that second interview, I had been too stupid to dodge the guns. But, now, oh yes, I was ready this time…

49

I went in for the interview to return to teaching. The living Thunderbird puppet – Maury Wilson – still looked and acted as if he'd been preserved in formaldehyde. He had stained crevasses around the corners of his mouth from his eerie grin.

"Hello there," he said at the college's entrance, slowly shifting into his phony grimace. Then came the overly strong handshake, and the accusing look straight into my eyes.

I met his gaze without blinking. As per his instructions, I'd had a long night sleep. I'd also had a hefty hit of gin followed by a lot of tooth brushing.

Wilson led me up to his office. It was the only place in the College where you had to walk up steps.

"I'm imagine you're wondering why we've taken so long to get in touch. We were concerned about our BTEC numbers."

I plonked on the midget seat yet again and my legs scrunched up. I said: "Alright…"

Academic

"It's lovely to see you again," he said, and grimaced. "How have things been, old chap?"

I squirmed in my tiny, low seat. I was still looking up at a guy who was six inches shorter than me. It should never have been disconcerting, but it was.

I went on about staying in New York and Norway. I cut out anything about Murder Slim and any failures. I said I was doing design work here and there, but I avoided how terribly it paid.

I remembered my new mantra: "Never talk too much."

Wilson smiled throughout but his eyes were disinterested. I thought of him rutting his Maths' teacher wife with the same dead expression on his face.

He flipped into business mode — a little adjustment of his glasses and a slight rise in his seat. Those were practiced movements from managerial seminars, along with the boring pauses where I was supposed to hang myself by jabbering on.

He said: "Well, it's been debated a lot behind the scenes."

Wilson paused for twenty seconds. I stayed quiet.

"You have many strengths: your students achieve the highest possible levels, you're an inspirational teacher…"

I tuned out and waited for the "but." In any sentence, nothing matters before the "but."

"But…" There you go. "You can be too controversial and ultimately…" and he finally said it: "You're not a team player."

I had to stop myself from laughing. This was writing GOLD. I made sure to jot down the conversation straight afterward.

"I've always helped teachers when they've asked for it." My defence mechanism and gut full of booze kicked in: "I've never needed to ask anyone for help. I deal with stuff with my students by myself." I shrugged: "I'm self-sufficient."

He paused for a couple of seconds then locked me with his dead-eyed stare: "Of course," he flashed his rigor-mortis smile, "but there's also the general feeling that you teach boys better than girls."

I smiled: "Do you have any statistics on that? My impression was that my students – male and female – got grades far above their other subjects. Among the best in the country... Often *the* best in the country."

"But it's rather well known you tend to teach somewhat," somehow it felt as if I had him on the ropes, "masculine films."

"Horror films are now watched by a roughly 50/50 split of men and women."

"Well..."

"So you raised the same problem with female teachers screening romantic comedies and alienating male students?"

Wilson crumbled slightly: "It's only an impression."

Shit, I was winning. Nothing like not giving a fuck to help...

Wilson looked down and put in five seconds of thought. Then he looked up again with a "fuck you" smirk: "And how is your alcohol problem?"

I flinched – wondering if he'd noticed a smell of gin: "I never had an alcohol problem."

Another pause, shorter than the last one.

"Well, let's give you the guided tour, old chap..."

50

After I was hired back as a BTEC Media and A Level Film teacher, I continued to focus on films that were deemed "common" by my fellow teachers. *Raiders of the Lost Ark*, *The Texas Chain-Saw Massacre*, *Barfly*, *Once Were Warriors*, *Dawn of the Dead* and so on.

This had nothing to do with masculinity. I picked them to rebel against how other Film tutors liked to watch dreary "social realist" films where they could gaze at working class stereotypes from a safe distance. Their favourite filmmakers had no directorial chops and little ability for realistic dialogue. Mike Leigh. Shane Meadows. Ken Loach. My fellow Film teacher was the worst of these: teaching *Secrets and Lies* alongside such false gems as Iranian cinema and fucking *Billy Elliot*.

As a perk of the Film course, we got to see the odd free movie. Local councils ran these for students and teachers. One year it was Shane Meadows' *Somers Town*.

At one particularly stupid moment – where a heavily overweight Cockney "Del-Boy" stereotype pulled money from his jockstrap – my fellow Film teacher exploded into laughter.

"HAR-HAR-HAR!"

I sat back in my seat. I was glad I had found somewhere in the screening room away from other people.

"HAR-HAR-HAR!!!" Her laughter was haughty but still genuine. Some of her students joined in.

But what was she laughing at? Would she laugh at a fat guy pulling money out of his jockstrap in real life? Or would she slap him and be vastly offended?

As we waited for the College's bus to pick us up, she asked: "What did you think of it...?"

"Not much," I said. "It was irritating and facile."

She looked stunned and a little sniffy: "But didn't you like the people *clinging onto humanity*... Surviving somehow...?"

This wasn't humanity. This was the middle class view of how the poor live. From the Northern runaway kid eating a Polish sausage and getting diarrhoea, to that Del-Boy character who was a shonky salesman of sun-chairs. All of it was in tediously grainy black-and-white. Realism, apparently, doesn't come in colour.

I was starting to twitch with frustration, wanting to explain all of that. But if I launched into some attack, it would travel around college within a day.

Every tiny action was magnified when you don't fit into a group. My tendency was to say the most inappropriate thing because I'm easily bored and edgy.

Booze always calmed me, while I'd learned to stay clear of coffee, cocaine and other stimulants.

Academic

Teachers stand around drinking endless cups of coffee, chain-smoking and dribbling over their choice of biscuits. But booze is an absolute no-no.

I resolved that vodka needed to be utilised when I knew I'd have to face teachers. Even if I could last just a year, my low overheads would meant I would clear a thousand quid or so.

But had I become what they had constructed me to be? An alcoholic?

I made sure to pick almost-odourless vodka and keep brushing my teeth with the strongest toothpaste I could find.

I told myself: "FOCUS, you fucktard. Keep to *the rules*."

51

After my previous teaching stint had driven me to near-insanity, I'd carefully figured out my rules for institutional survival…

1. Always looks busy and walk quickly. If you see a teacher sidling towards you, wave cheerily and take a different route.

2. If cornered and asked about your life and views, reverse the question and then leave as soon as they've finished yapping. Never, EVER, say an unkind word to a female teacher.

3. Sit in a toilet during busy staffroom periods. Always check your pigeonhole during the middle of lessons.

4. Never talk during staff meetings unless prompted. If prompted, seem confused yet affable. Never talk too much.

5. Never compromise your teaching style. Students aren't your enemy. If they like you, they're forgiving and accommodating.

Between lessons, I moved into the staff toilet and read a book. That could last a good hour because the staff/disabled toilet was largely unused. On the rare occasion another teacher had dropped their load, that smell was preferable to hearing the same waste spout from their mouths.

I had no thought of promotion or a career, much as I didn't want a wife or a family. All I wanted was to teach lessons to the best of my ability and have the opportunity to read or watch or write stuff.

But teaching never works out like that, and Donna was the first profound kick to the nuts in my second tour of duty.

Donna was the other BTEC Media teacher and is among the most evil people I've known. She was 50 years old and a rusty blade of horror. She wasn't a serial killer – I haven't known any of those – but she was another nervous breakdown away from slitting throats. My German teacher at school had sobbed out of despair, but Donna poured her near-lunacy into a need to destroy.

It wasn't hard to see why my bosses were worried about the BTEC course. Wilson hadn't lied there... the issue genuinely wasn't with hiring me as a lowly serf, but some calculation about whether the course could sustain itself.

Five students were enrolled on the course. FIVE. A standard class is 20 or so, yet this course existed with five. A practical and "fun" course, where students got the chance to make movies...

Ah, Donna. After two minutes you knew she was the reason it was failing. The kids despised Donna. They labelled her a lesbian (she wasn't) and visibly withered when she was around.

Donna had taught the group for a year, reducing the number of students from 12 to 5. Three girls and two guys had survived – *Jewel:* heavily overweight and very smart, rarely had praise because people fixated on her weight. *Rhoda:* wildly sarcastic and defensive, secretly negative about herself. *Kerry:* very tall, self-consciously ditsy and eager to please. *Gary:* a fostered kid now living alone... intense, quiet, angry. *Jack:* fun-loving guy with ambitions to carve a career spray-painting cars.

They were normal students. Each year was filled with individuals like these, all with fuck-ups and upsides. Around 90% of kids could be reached in some way, if only by saying nice things or being the first to challenge their prejudices. Most *wanted* to like their teacher and the *vast* majority were great kids finding their way.

It's very seldom that you change students. Long term, you change one out of twenty. But you changed all of them for the time they were in your lesson. This was a minuscule part of their lives, so it was important to try and make it memorable. As much as anything, education gave them time to breathe before a grinding job and a demanding family kicked in. I hoped to help them think, to see other things... even only for an hour per weekday.

Above all, I liked my students, for all their occasional anger or bone-headedness. I liked listening about their relationships and their home-lives. As a teacher, I was a paid friend as well as a paid educator. I loved seeing even the briefest glimpse of progress.

In contrast, Donna didn't like her students. She *hated* them. It's not a word I throw around. She wouldn't plan lessons. She would throw together movie clips minutes before she had to teach. She spent her free time bitching how Rhoda was selfish, Kerry was stupid, Jewel was fat and lazy, Jack was a "chav," and that Gary would kill us. I broke a couple of rules and defended them. Her shit-stream of hatred could break through anything.

Donna was the embodiment of the secret thoughts that too many teachers have. An increasing sense of superiority over their students coupled with a simmering dislike of them. A bad lesson was always the students' fault. Bad results were always the exam board's fault. And all that bad stuff could always find a tone-deaf ear with other teachers whining about the same thing.

The staff room had older teachers on easy-chairs, drinking coffee and moaning about problem students. The younger teachers sat on the eight computers, drinking lattes and yakking about the same issues as they posted Facebook messages.

All of them were hopped up on a caffeine fuelled power trip and, in their own way, they were all desperate to fit in.

52

I will admit – out of that first year of BTEC – Rhoda *could* be hard work. She was sniffy with a low attention span.

But that sort of thing should fire the teacher to speed up their lessons. Lessons need a sense of rhythm. It was easy to accommodate for this when I taught Media or Film. I made sure to show a movie clip every ten minutes. It gave the students a mental break, and it forced me to split the lesson into paragraphs.

One Wednesday, I'd waffled too much and sensed how boring I had become. The BTEC course was work orientated, so I asked them how their jobs were going.

Kerry was cleaning caravans. Jack was living his dream and learning about paint mixtures in a garage. Jewel was a glass collector in a shitty pub. Gary wasn't in work, but as a fostered kid he needed to attend college for 90% of his lessons to receive money from the government.

Rhoda – now alert after she'd been given the chance to talk about her life – was working for a large newsagent.

"How is it?" I asked.

"I hate it. It's stupid," she crossed her eyes. "Stoo-pid!"

"Tell 'im 'bout yer boss," Kerry said.

"Is he a scary fucker?" I said.

"Nah, not that. Not really. He's a dick though…" She thought for a second. "I'll be working, like, in the basement bit. But I never do it quick enough for him. He likes to shout. I mean he really does!"

"Welcome to the world of bosses."

Rhoda's eyes became dreamy. "But I still love him."

"What?"

Kerry was laughing already, and Rhoda slapped her arm. Gary, Jack and Jewel were quiet but honed in on the conversation.

"I love him. He's well fit."

"What?"

"And he's got a nice car too. It din 'ave a roof! He let me sit in it once!" Kerry started to laugh, and Rhoda joined in: "Fuck off, I'd totally do him! I would!"

Maybe I was tired, but it annoyed me hugely. I took a few deep breaths, but they didn't help. I tried to structure my response into something that would come across as a joke.

"You know what the problem with the world is?" No response. The students were suddenly quiet. I shouted: "TOO MANY CUNTS FUCKING DICKHEADS!"

I smiled to try and prompt the laughs, but the students looked scared. Even the uber-upbeat Kerry was forward and behind me.

Academic

I slowly looked over my right shoulder. There, in the doorway from the computer room, was Donna. She was a timeless academic stereotype... a modern-day Mrs. McKay. She was furiously attempting to try to chug smoke out her ears.

Donna harrumphed loudly: "I'll leave you with this SEXIST." She stormed out. I looked back at the group and met their smiles. Jack's and Gary's were the widest, but they'd misinterpreted what I had said...

What I had said WASN'T sexist, but I knew it was pointless chasing after Donna and telling her that. I knew I couldn't change the minds of teachers, but I did enjoy telling the students the truth. I sat down and said: "Flip the words around in what I just said. 'Too many dickheads fucking cunts.' Donna would STILL find that sexist to women, even though I'm attacking both genders."

Maybe it was too easy to put Donna down. I fed into the students' dislike of her, but I never pretended to be her friend. In teaching that's rare. They creep around each other. So many had dreams of more money, their own office, and – if they played their cards correctly – no actual teaching.

Donna wanted to redress injustices that existed 30 years ago. Yet again, that fed into a new wave of pointless injustices...

That incident – along with many others – confirmed one of the weird biases of teaching. The profession is now vastly outnumbered by female to male teachers. Out of my bosses, eighty-five percent were female. Out of the total teachers in college, there was an 80/20 split from female to male. In primary school, where young minds suck up much more, the split was touching 90/10.

The prominent shift towards female teachers isn't accidental. Many male teachers are forced out the profession early on, caught in "sex scandals." These are sometimes true, sometimes bogus. But they are always taken with deadly seriousness and manufactured into truth through the gossip mill.

I actually heard more confirmed rumours about female teachers fucking male students. These were often passed off as male students making up stories or "grooming" their teacher. In teaching, women are typically cast in the role of both victim and superior.

It's not hard to figure out where this comes from. After hundreds of years of moronic male domination, feminism has rightly searched for equality. But it's now pushed beyond. Female teachers and students know they can't be challenged by guys because they can stick the "sexist" tag onto them.

Donna said, in another bone-headed exchange: "Teaching horror films again, then...."

"Yep. *Day of the Dead* this year. I fancied a change."

"You do realise they're sexist," she sneered, "don't you?"

"Huh?"

"Even the *final girl* archetype just gives male viewers the chance to voyeuristically watch the female heroine suffer."

I said: "Horror is forward thinking. That's what I teach my students."

I could have named tens of horror films that pushed against negative stereotypes of gender. But what was the point?

I kept to the rules and remained a closed book. Yet even I couldn't smile as the other Film teacher once said: "Oh, you're such a *m-a-n*..."

53

Donna lasted for three further years. It felt like an eternity, but it didn't entirely crush my job. I liked the vast majority of my students without having to try.

By being a part-time teacher, my interaction with Donna was limited enough that I still enjoyed each workday. I only had to deal with her twice a month in tedious meetings about the (now suddenly expanding) BTEC course and to check whether we were marking essays evenly.

Thankfully, even fuckwit teachers had largely taken a dislike to Donna. Face-to-face they were pleasant to her, but they bitched loudly behind her back.

I dodged any trouble from the couple of outbursts I did have. There was one argument over restructuring the movie trailer unit. I wanted to veer it towards horror because it is a genre that can have real power even with tiny amounts of money. *Re-Animator, Brain Damage, Combat Shock, Street Trash, Evil Dead...*

Academic

Donna wanted them to make Westerns. *Westerns?* There are great westerns, but how can kids work in that genre with a £20 budget? She equated challenging genres as good for the kids.

I dug my heels in and she dug into a rant at me: "EVERYTHING HAS TO BE DONE YOUR WAY! THIS IS WHAT THEY NEED TO DO! IT WILL MAKE THEM THINK FOR A CHANGE!"

I shook violently. Outside of college I would have flipped, but I dutifully bit my lip. She stormed off again, like one of the teens she seemed to find so petulant.

Urgh... I looked at another college door slowly easing shut on its safety device. After that, the silence meant my shaking subsided too.

When I was told Donna was leaving college – after knowing that teaching contracts meant she could never be fired – it was like taking the first breath of air after being released from jail.

It said something about my new found sense of control that I had made it through Donna without drawing attention to my hatred of her.

A sell out? Fuck that. You choose the battles you can win. You also win by the freedom it gives you at other times. Saying nothing wasn't giving in, but lying would have been.

You can't directly fight against teachers. The sheer weight of numbers doesn't allow for it. But, hey, it didn't stop me from having fun with them now and then...

54

In the spirit of exploration, I tried to see teachers at play. Sure, they seemed overly tetchy, but the job did have its pressures... catch anyone on a bad day and they can snap.

I went along to the Christmas party that year.

It wasn't because I couldn't avoid the damn event – I'd avoided it for over a decade – but because I wanted to see what happened at them.

It was held in one of the large meeting rooms. No booze, of course. The food was served by the canteen staff, and there were long queues for the two coffee machines set to "free vend."

The atmosphere was suitably odd. Happy and seemingly relaxed, yet slightly stilted and unreal. There was tinsel hung around the staid teaching furniture and four carollers (elderly Music teachers) loudly singing out-of-tune Christmas hymns.

The teachers sat exclusively according to their subjects. They talked in hushed voices. Lower-level bosses sat with their departments, while higher bosses sat on a table by themselves. The hum and laughter of conversation flowed around me.

I felt uncomfortable straight away. I was out of my depth trapped by so many teachers. I took a lot of trips to the toilet but I never ran away. I was too scared to draw attention to myself by just disappearing. Like some autistic kid, I had years to develop practiced responses to a bunch of stuff I didn't care about.

The conversation on my Media/Film/Communication Studies' table was about the usual things. Unruly students (again).

Coffee and biscuits (again). Then a huge amount of overly positive stuff about their progenies. How Joshua was great at fucking rugby, or how Anastasia had learned to speak so fucking quickly, or how Barnaby loved studying at fucking Cambridge.

I used my rules once again – reversing their questions whenever possible. Another Media teacher asked: "So, how is your mother getting on?"

"Well, you know..." I breathed out slowly. "But tell me more about Barnaby's course?"

I only cracked once. The other Film teacher talked about her daughter – Anouska – and how she wanted to see a "15" rated movie for the first time: "She's only 14, but she particularly wants to see *Black Swan*. And..." she leaned in to whisper into my ear, "...I was going to smuggle her in because she's so mature for her age. As you know, I adore *Aronofsky*." She said his name with real arousal. "Unfortunately, I listened to Mark Kermode's review and he said there is a somewhat explicit lesbian sex scene..."

I acted startled. As I did it, I sickened myself. She laughed at whatever expression my face pulled. She said: "Not that it's remotely a problem of course!" She looked to one side: "It's just that wouldn't it be dreadfully awkward watching that together?"

With four slugs of vodka inside me and tired of the whole event, I said: "Couldn't you just slide your hand behind her and say: 'Honey, there's something I always meant to tell you?'"

She slapped my arm and rasped: "DON'T BE FILTHY!" and conversation stalled on the table. I decided to take another whizz.

Academic

As I walked back, the psychadelic David Lynch mood was completed by a Maths' teacher who was reading poems about each teaching department. He was dressed as Santa Claus, and had each of his limericks written on different coloured cards.

He was a lovable "old school" eccentric with a wide gut and a sense of optimism, but the guy wasn't a poet. Who is? As he rattled them off, I concentrated on trying to smile as the other teachers erupted into self-conscious laughter.

I went to the toilet again after the Media/Film limerick and frantically wrote down his ditty on Film Studies.

"There once was a student called Jim,

"Who couldn't concentrate due to a whim,

"He only wanted to watch TV,

"As much as he could see-see,

"So he settled on studying Film."

Yes, I was baffled by the "see-see" too.

I went back into battle and behaved beautifully...

55

By that time, I was 34 and I could count at least sixty people who had a role they considered superior to my teaching post. A standard teacher is almost outnumbered by their bosses.

Academic

First, there was "additional responsibility." They got paid an extra grand for dealing with a lot of extra paperwork. They were second in command to the "Head of Department" (HOD).

HOD was sub-divided into subject groups: English, Media, Maths, Science, History, Geography, Performance Studies etc. They could be Head of Department (£3000-£6000 extra per year) even if they only had one other teacher in their department.

"Senior Tutor." There were one of those for every ten teachers. My college had fifteen. They procured their own office and dealt – usually badly – with troublesome students.

"Head of Curriculum." There were six of those, and they were Head of Department Heads. As a Media/Film teacher, my curriculum group was Media/Business/I.T.

Next up the greasy pole was "Deputy Principal". You'd think they would have been one of those, but there were three. One Science based, one Arts based, one Humanities based.

All carrots led towards the role as head-honcho. Principal. £120,000+ a year. No teaching. A personal secretary. It isn't hard to wonder what is required to get that far. Almost all principals are over 50, and haven't taught full-time for more than ten years.

The younger teachers strove to "climb the ladder," while older teachers got very sniffy when they didn't get promoted.

The Shane Meadows' obsessed Film teacher was particularly peeved not to get a Senior Tutor position. She ranted about it in meetings, even though it entailed a bunch of paperwork far in excess of monetary reward. The goal was purely to be promoted. *Dominate students. Buy Anouska more stuff.*

This led to a bunch of revolting activities.

Firstly, there were voluntary tasks… selling the college at open evenings and education fayres. They were tolerable enough, and didn't require lying. I'd pitch Film Studies – the good and the bad – and most would pick up the course.

Secondly, though, there were college-based parties. Something akin to a noisy gathering in Hell. Maury Wilson's son was an adept trumpet player, and Wilson would organise trumpet recitals where teachers could appreciate his son's talent. These would be attended by twenty or so teachers. Maybe they were all lovers of brass music?

Climbing the ladder deflected the focus from putting time into good lessons.

And how the fuck do you think it made the students feel?

56

I had now spent eight more years teaching after my return. All of the workdays gave me the nights to write, act as a carer for my mother, and post books for fans of Murder Slim Press.

I had long periods of marking essays, but also long holidays. It certainly beat the shit out of barwork. A good lesson was wonderful... like a stand-up comedian when the audience laughs at every joke. When a lesson worked, I felt a surge of happiness. The job was occasionally frustrating, but it was often fucking fun.

Sadly, my final abiding memory is a shitty one. Every few months, I was subjected to group training. Motivational speakers yapped about how to modernise teaching.

That training was "Equal Opportunities." A noble cause, at least, but dealt with the usual ham-fisting that feels like your anus might prolapse.

I stupidly broke one of my minor rules by turning up early to the damn event. I headed for an empty table, sat in peace for five minutes, before having nine idiot teachers come and sit with me. I found a couple of them particularly objectionable. The backstabbing Dance teacher and the laddish Music Technology teacher. I should have dug a fucking hole or turned into a ghost...

The Music Tech teacher had a thing for the Dance teacher, so I got a close-up view of his desperate, sycophantic flirting. He whispered in her ear and giggled. She was on the verge of "settling." He was heavily overweight, but she was hitting her mid-thirties. She wanted kids and the herd of sperm donors was thinning at an alarming rate. She whispered back into his ear...

After a one-hour diatribe defining Equal Opportunities and establishing words that were no longer acceptable ("deaf," "blind" and "gay" were amongst those), each table was given a different issue to deal with.

Academic

We were given the following: *"You are passing out condom-cards* [n.b. – that's a genuinely heroic idea where kids get free condoms] *to your class. As you go to pass out the last card to a female student, a male student shouts out 'DON'T MIND 'ER... SHE'S SAVING IT FOR JESUS."*

Aside from the Dance and Music Tech teachers who were still busy with their verbal dry humping, the other teachers on the table were indignant. They wanted to stop their lesson. They wanted to lecture the male student. They wanted to SHOW the rest of the group how wrong his comment was.

I had taken another big swig of vodka beforehand, knowing how objectionable the training would be. So I said: "I wouldn't stop the lesson. I'd have a word with the kid afterwards. You stop the lesson and you make the girl feel like shit." I hated the lack of misunderstanding from the uber-feminist teachers. Didn't they understand? "It makes her the focus of attention. By getting pissy over the comment, you exaggerate the power of an offhand joke."

I didn't win, of course. The two teachers next to me sniffed. I had sworn and said something *unprofessional*. The rest of the table eventually followed suit.

Oh, fuck this nonsense...

We reached the "plenary" stage, where you had to relate your findings to the room of 150 teachers. The faces kept changing but their beliefs didn't.

Academic

I looked around. I was now one of the last teachers who were still there from almost fifteen years ago. The stupidity remained. It didn't amplify. *It just was.*

Teachers don't learn. *And that was what I learned.*

A middle-aged, middle-upper class teacher called Charlotte stood up to give her group's plenary: "We were given the following dilemma: 'A girl in your class seems to be agitated. A male student shouts out: *'Don't mind her. She's on the blob!'* We were requested to see how we'd deal with the situation."

In a room full of 80% female teachers, I waited.

Charlotte looked around and smiled: "When this sort of event happens, I like to respond with wit, not intelligence." There were a few laughs from the room. "I like to tell the boy that men are full of testosterone. It's proven that they think about sex every seven seconds."

Thirty or so teachers applauded. The vast majority of the rest of the room laughed, and I wanted to bonk my head on the table.

This female dominated world was as stupid as the male dominated world of the 50s. A world where sexism towards guys was celebrated. Where teachers loved the working class, as long as they were kept at a safe distance. Where they claimed to celebrate the power of learning, yet practised the dark arts of social climbing.

57

I have written for so many nights for so many years. Lanny, Deanna, Wilson, Donna, Thomas and reams more. I wrote down everything I felt, trying to find some pattern to it. Surely I could learn something from this mess of experiences?

Drunkenness, women, teaching, fights. Hundreds and thousands of people write similar stories for small magazines, publishers and – these days – websites. I think that only three of them can write for shit, but how many see that? One in ten thousand? One in a million? Stick a few "fucks" in a story they'll always be other fucks who will lap at it like a honey-coated clit...

How I am better than that?

Over the years, my skills improved enough that I found some success. I still write now, drawing all the life out of twenty years of academia. I'm lucky that there's still energy left in them. I'm lucky to still be alive.

I write about the past because the distance gives it safety. It's truth, but not the whole truth.

So I better tell you when I quit the first time, I had became agoraphobic. Once again, I can't blame it on Deanna, although that fed into how I turned inward through knowledge and fear.

I became someone who took everything, every moment, every nuance, seriously. I was the guy who used to cut himself with a razor-sharp pair of scissors just to find some clarity and relief through the blood running from his chest.

Academic

The role of teacher can be like a disease. If you spend too much time around them, you can catch the damn thing.

All of that ridiculous sarcasm, the mind-numbing gossip, the prissy attitude...

I saw young teachers catch it within two years. Over-elaborate words sank like an over-sized depth-charge into their conversations and their teaching. *Professionalism* became their watchword. Along with that came the need for the bigger TV, the bigger car, the bigger house. They visibly yearned for acknowledgment from their peers and promotion...

"Career" became "Life."

I chose to go back there, and I'll concede there must have been other free-thinking teachers at college. But I only met one: the aptly named "Cheri." The effort required to find the rest was too risky. By sticking to my rules, I was reticent around all of them and kept my thoughts in check. I never cut myself again...

It meant I pulled in enough money for the time needed to do the things I enjoyed. All of that side of my life involved some cock-eyed belief in the truth... against a world that revered fiction.

My writing consistently veers into rants, where repressed emotions pour out. *Fuck, have I still become like them by bitching about them in this story?*

The role has a weird power, and it infects just as much as it heals. It's a word that's revered, because we remember the best of them instead of the grinding majority.

Academic

But I did learn something:
"Teacher." That word can become your life.
So run, fucking RUN away...
And – eventually – I did.

Afterword
by Seymour Shubin

Steve Hussy was in his twenties when, quite happily, he quit teaching at a college. Put it all behind him. Or so he thought. A few years later, a business associate having screwed him, he applied for a part-time position at the same college, which at one time he'd hoped he would never see again. Perhaps to his surprise, but more likely theirs -- for he had been known to be his own man -- they took him back.

Lucky for them. And lucky for the students who were to come into his life. And, oh yes, lucky for us.

The college got themselves one hell of a teacher. And we have in hand one hell of a writer.

Mr. Hussy, now 34, teaches media and film courses. He helps his students, almost all of whom come from low-income families, make films rather than simply analyze them. And he speaks their "language." For instance he swears, he says, "more than is acceptable." (Readers will vouch for that, but I hope it will be the unusual one who won't accept it as part of a true story.) For instance, in his classroom, "Say what you like about fart and sex jokes. They don't truly demean like sarcasm does. That's why I banned it in my classroom."

Funny, yes. And true.

Mr. Hussy is not unsparing in offering his feelings -- mostly dislikes -- of teachers and, indeed, the "system." The only thing wrong with teaching, he maintains, are the teachers.

But he is hardly a misanthrope.

"I learned to love teaching," he says, which is a far cry from that young man who couldn't wait to quit.

Mr. Hussy has plenty to say about the change, which alone would make this story must reading.

I offer a hearty thanks for showing us why.

And for doing it so well -- and entertainingly.

Seymour Shubin
Philadelphia, 2011

WE ARE GLASS by u.v. ray

"u.v. ray is by turns passionate, angered, insightful and rebellious... Great writing removes the lid from the rotting can, it challenges the false and empty symbol. u.v. ray does that with aplomb."
---Richard Godwin (author of *Mr. Glamour*), Introduction to *We Are Glass*

"u.v. ray's *We Are Glass* is a must have. Buy it, consume it, and ask for seconds. I did."
---Adam Campbell, *9Sense Podcast*

Trade paperback size
167 pages

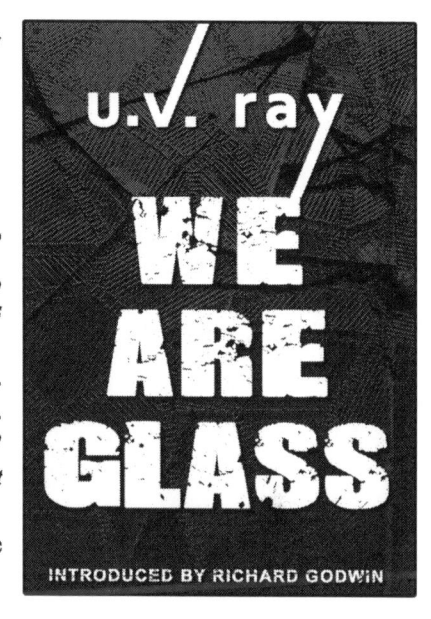

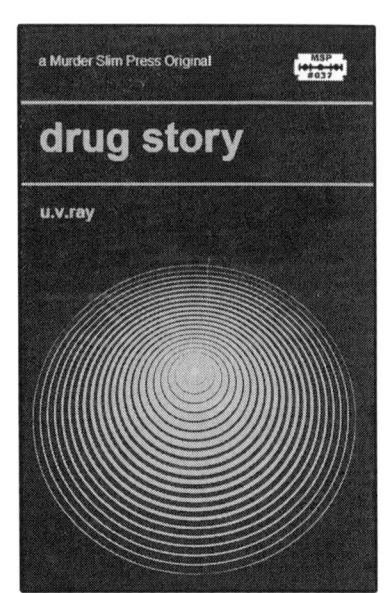

DRUG STORY by u.v. ray

"If you lived a life of abuse and excess, you know how bitterly honest this book is, and yet it almost makes you yearn for those moments of depravity and madness again."
--- Adam Campbell, *Speak of the Devil*

"A story of the ages... relevant and seminal in its capacity to shock and shake us to the core."
--- *Angry Today*

"Great book, if you're brave enough to read it."
--- Gil De Ray

Vintage paperback size
207 pages

murder slim press
since 2004
writing at the razor's edge
murderslim.com

THE MIGRANT by u.v. ray

"u.v.ray's novella, *The Migrant*, wasn't written to make us feel all warm and fuzzy, this is off the scale uncomfortable and from deep in the gut, the best kind of writing always is. His poetry and thoughts fly into the night, the search for human connection, he knows his place within the stars and time, believes in nothing, embracing his foibles, his anger and vision of the world."
--- Abbie Foxton, *Abbie Foxton.com*

Limited to 200 Copies
Best Novella Saboteur Award Nominee
Chapbook size / 110 pages

SAINT OF THE CITY by David Noone

"It is certainly noir fiction with both poise and purpose, not something you can really have too much of in the contemporary canon. [It's] a scaborous little tale, swift and compulsive in the telling, which manages to pack a lot of points into a svelte amount of pages."
--- Cathi Unsworth, Introduction to *Saint of the City*

"For all its relative brevity, the tremors left behind are visceral and unsettling."
--- Christopher Brownsword, *Empty Mirror*

Limited to 300 Copies / 110 pages

murder slim press
since 2004
writing at the razor's edge
murderslim.com

THE SAVAGE KICK #5
featuring:
Ivan Brunetti: Interview & **Cartoons** /
Another Tough Time by **Mark SaFranko** /
Deadly Spanking by **Jim Hanley** / *First*
by **Steve Hussy** / *Slut, Bitch, Whore* by
Julie Kazimer / **Seymour Shubin**:
Interview & *Lonely No More* / *Worse Feeling There Is* by **Robert McGowan** /
Bloody Virtue by **Jeffrey Bacon** / *Carl of Hollyweird* by **Kevin O'Kendley** /
Halloween by **J.R. Helton** / **Joe R. Lansdale**: Interview & *One Of Them* /
SK's Picks of 2009 / Cover by **Richard Watts** / 10 Pages of Art by **Steve Hussy**

Triple sized / 232 pages

THE SAVAGE KICK #6
featuring:
Dan Fante: Interview & **Point Doom** excerpt
Dead To Rights by **Seymour Shubin**
The First Flower by **u.v. ray**
Slug by **Steve Hussy**
Debbie Drechsler: Interview & *Daddy Knows Best* / *The Target* by **Kevin O'Kendley**
Headache by **William Hart**
Innocent by **Aaron Garrison**
Prison Prose by **Jeffrey Frye**
Morning by **Matthew Wilding**
Things That Weren't True by **Rob McGowan**
Savage Kick's Picks of 2010 and 2011
Cover & 12 Pages of Art by **Steve Hussy**

Triple sized / 206 pages

murder slim press
since 2004 — writing at the razor's edge
murderslim.com

BANK BLOGGER by Jeffrey P. Frye

"When I told people that I planned to rob banks and intentionally get sent to prison so I could get my own blog, people looked at me like I was crazy. Well who looks crazy now?"
---Jeffrey Frye, USP Resident

9 short stories including
7 exclusive tales not on the
Bloggie-nominated *Bank Robber's Blog*
9 pages of exclusive photographs

Limited to 200 Copies
Chapbook size
78 pages

ONE CRAZY DAY by Jeffrey P. Frye

"In *One Crazy Day*, which follows his debut *Bank Blogger*, Frye tells the crazy story of his last robbery. You want sex, insanity, excitement? *One Crazy Day* delivers all that. Like in *Bank Blogger*, his writing is lean and straight to the point, almost Bukowskian, but infused with great comic relief. "A truly unique new voice in American literature."
---Rasmus Drews, *Amazon*

Limited to 200 Copies
Chapbook size
70 pages

murder slim press
since 2004
writing at the razor's edge
murderslim.com

***THE HUNCH* by Seymour Shubin**

"Seymour fills his books with genuine emotion and small human touches... as well as keen psychological insights. *The Hunch* is... gripping and haunting [because] the anguish and trauma that this couple go through are genuine and heartfelt."
---Dave Zeltserman (author of *Pariah*), Introduction to *The Hunch*

"Seymour Shubin is a great crime author... [and] the novel is a delight to read."
---Rod Loft, *Bookgasm*

Trade paperback size
184 pages

***LONELY NO MORE* by Seymour Shubin**

"As you're swept into the momentum of any given tale, it's easy to overlook all of his other considerable strengths: he's incredibly perceptive, touching, funny, compassionate and versatile, among a whole host of other qualities. I can't think of any higher compliment that can be paid to a master."
--- Mark SaFranko (author of *Hating Olivia*), Introduction to *Lonely No More*

Art by **Richard Watts** and **Steve Hussy**

Trade paperback size
126 pages

murder slim press
since 2004
writing at the razor's edge
murderslim.com

Murder Slim Press: Checklist

- MSP#000 – *The Savage Kick #1* ft. Dan Fante ☐
- MSP#001 – *Hating Olivia* by Mark SaFranko ☐
- MSP#002 – *Role of A Lifetime* by Mark SaFranko ☐
- MSP#003 – *The Savage Kick #2* ft. Doug Stanhope ☐
- MSP#004 – *The Savage Kick #3* ft. Jim Goad ☐
- MSP#005 – *Steps* by Steve Hussy ☐
- MSP#006 – *The Angel* by Tommy Trantino ☐
- MSP#007 – The Savage Kick #4 ft. Joe Matt ☐
- MSP#008 – *Lounge Lizard* by Mark SaFranko ☐
- MSP#009 – *Loners* by Mark SaFranko ☐
- MSP#010 – *Life Change* by Mark SaFranko ☐
- MSP#011 – *Savage Kick #5* by Mark SaFranko ☐
- MSP#012 – *The Hunch* by Seymour Shubin ☐
- MSP#013 – *God Bless America* by Mark SaFranko ☐
- MSP#014 – *Lonely No More* by Seymour Shubin ☐
- MSP#015 – *The Savage Kick #6* ft. Debbie Drechsler ☐
- MSP#016 – *NAM* by Robert McGowan ☐
- MSP#017 – *A Long Perambulation* by Robert McGowan ☐
- MSP#018 – *We Are Glass* by u.v. ray ☐
- MSP#019 – *Bank Blogger* by Jeffrey P. Frye ☐
- MSP#020 – *Why Me?* by Seymour Shubin ☐
- MSP#021 – *One Crazy Day* by Jeffrey P. Frye ☐
- MSP#022 – *Spiral Out* by u.v. ray ☐
- MSP#023 – *Dirty Work* by Mark SaFranko ☐
- MSP#024 – *The Captain* by Seymour Shubin ☐
- MSP#025 – *The Savage Kick #7* ft. Carson Mell ☐
- MSP#026 – *The Migrant* by u.v. ray ☐
- MSP#027 – *Back* by Steve Hussy ☐
- MSP#028 – *Sometimes You Just...* by Mark SaFranko ☐
- MSP#029 – *The Artistic Life* by Mark SaFranko ☐
- MSP#030 – *South Main Stories* by Robert McGowan ☐
- MSP#031 – *Black Cradle* by u.v. ray ☐
- MSP#032 – *Saint Of The City* by David Noone ☐
- MSP#033 – *The Savage Kick #8* ft. Cathi Unsworth ☐
- MSP#034 – *The Savage Kick #9* ft. Mark SaFranko ☐
- MSP#035 – *Blossoms and Blood* by Mark SaFranko ☐
- MSP#036 – *The Savage Kick #10* ft. Willy Vlautin ☐
- MSP#037 – *Drug Story* by u.v. ray ☐
- MSP#038 – *Little Miss Awesome* by Steve Hussy ☐
- MSP#039 – *Little Miss Awesome* by Ally North ☐

murder slim press
since 2004
writing at the razor's edge
murderslim.com

Printed in Poland
by Amazon Fulfillment
Poland Sp. z o.o., Wrocław